THE CHAMBER OF FIVE

MICHAEL HARMON

THE CHAMBER OF FIVE

ALFRED A. KNOPF

NEW YORK

THIS IS A BORZOI BOOK PUBLISHED BY ALFRED A. KNOPF

All rights reserved. Published in the United States by Alfred A. Knopf, an imprint of Random House Children's Books, a division of Random House, Inc., New York.

Knopf, Borzoi Books, and the colophon are registered trademarks of Random House, Inc.

Visit us on the Web! www.randomhouse.com/teens

Educators and librarians, for a variety of teaching tools, visit us at www.randomhouse.com/teachers

Library of Congress Cataloging-in-Publication Data
Harmon, Michael B.
The Chamber of Five / Michael Harmon. — 1st ed.
p. cm.
Summary: When seventeen-year-old Jason Weatherby, the son of a congressman, is invited to join the secretive Chamber of Five, an elite group of students who run Lambert School for the Gifted via a shadow government, he sees how corrupt the institution is and decides to work from the inside to take it down when things go too far.
ISBN 978-0-375-86644-9 (trade) — ISBN 978-0-375-96644-6 (lib. bdg.) —
ISBN 978-0-375-89641-5 (ebook)
[1. Revenge—Fiction. 2. Politics, Practical—Fiction. 3. Schools—Fiction.
4. Family problems—Fiction.] I. Title.
PZ7.H22723Ch 2011
[Fic]—dc22
2010021077

The text of this book is set in 11-point Goudy.

Printed in the United States of America
June 2011
10 9 8 7 6 5 4 3 2 1
First Edition

For Sydney and Dylan

CHAPTER ONE

CARTER LOGAN LOUNGED in one of the brass-studded and leather-backed reading chairs in the study hall like a king drunk on his own power. The kind of power I'd grown up around, and the kind I didn't have much use for. With his tie loosened and his pressed white dress shirt untucked under his uniform sweater, he watched me walk in as I wondered again why I didn't have the strength to stand up for what I believed in.

The Joseph T. Lambert School for the Gifted study hall looked more like the cigar room at the Lidgerwood Country Club, which my father was a preferred member of, and Carter fit right in. Smoke and mirrors, I reminded myself. It's all smoke and mirrors.

Carter scratched his ear, hooking a leg over the arm of the leather-bound chair and slouching further into the padded thing. We were alone, the doors closed, a freshman stationed out in the hall guarding the entrance. "Hello, Jason."

I nodded, sitting across from him. "Carter."

He studied me for a moment, his eyes black pools. "It's a high position."

"Yeah, it is," I answered.

He smiled, speaking easy and soft, his thin lips moving precisely. "I've got to admit, most guys don't need more than a blink to accept." He eyed me. "It's been two days."

I'd already been chosen last year, my sophomore year, to be a member of the Youth Leadership Group, thirty-three members strong, and I thought that was enough. Nothing was ever enough, though, and now I was up for the holiest of the holy, a position in the Chamber of Five. Five guys chosen to oversee the Youth Leadership Group, and the school.

And like I said, you didn't just sign up for these groups, you were chosen. And the guy sitting in front of me was the chooser. The mysterious and infamous Carter Logan, president of the Chamber of Five.

With my selection last year into the Youth Leadership Group, my father had told every friend he had at the club before I'd even accepted. And now, a year later, I was sitting here with the king. They officially call it the presidency, but there was nothing democratic about it. Carter held the power. The rest of the Chamber simply filled chairs. With my mind returning to the conversation at hand, I shrugged. "I haven't thought much about it."

He leaned his head back, staring at the burnished beams of the ceiling. "Decisiveness is the key to leadership, Jason, and this school is about leadership. You should know that. Your father is a congressman for this great state."

Most everything that came out of Carter Logan's mouth was

tinged with lazy sarcasm, and he twirled his finger, still staring at the ceiling, when he said it. He bled confidence, oozed charm, reeked of intimidation.

I looked to the closed doors. The doors separating real life and the life I'd been born into. Smoke and mirrors. It doesn't matter what you think you are, my father had told me a dozen times. It matters only what others think you are. It dictated success, defeat, and the future. The golden key to politics was to be what they wanted you to be.

It was how he'd become a Washington State legislator with his eye on senator in the future. It was also how he'd become such a jerk.

My dad was like a thousand-pound octopus wrapped around my life, and having a screwup for a son when you were a politician wasn't acceptable. I sighed. The Chamber. I had to admit that the position with the Chamber, along with my dad's influence, would nail down admission into any Ivy League college I'd like. And more importantly, it would get my dad off my back.

I knew all the good reasons, all the ways that the Chamber would open doors to more opportunity and choice. The problem was that there wasn't an ounce of desire in me to be what I was supposed to be. Another problem was that when I looked in the mirror, I didn't see anybody I liked.

I shook my head, blinking. None of it mattered anyway. I'd take it because if I didn't, the biggest dog of hell would be unleashed in the form of my dad not only ripping off my head and crapping down my neck, but doing it repeatedly for the rest of the year. "I'll take it."

Carter nodded like I was a three-year-old kid who'd wiped

his ass without getting any on his hands. "Good. We'll see you tomorrow at four, then. The first meeting of the five will convene in the Chamber."

I stood, starting for the doors, then stopped. I looked back at him. "Hey, Carter?"

He turned his head, looking at me. "Yes?"

"Did I have a choice?"

He smiled. "Of course not, Jason. Who would turn down the Chamber?"

Me, I thought, if I wasn't a big pussy. "Then why did you even ask me?"

This time, he laughed. An easy and friendly thing that was almost infectious, and that almost made me feel like we were friends. "If I didn't know you better, Jason, I'd think you actually contemplated turning it down."

"You don't know me better, Carter."

He chuckled. "I know *who* you are, Jason. That's enough."

As I opened the doors and walked down the hall, I glanced at my watch. Twenty after three. I stepped up my pace, hitching my pack further on my shoulder and hustling to make tennis practice by three-thirty. Coach Yount would bitch anybody up one wall and down the other if they were late.

"Hey."

I slowed, turning, and Talbott Presley, otherwise known as Elvis, windmilled his disjointed and too-long legs after me. We'd been friends for a year, and I liked him because he was so incredibly smart that he didn't know the first thing about being social. He was brilliantly retarded, but he knew it and kept trying not to be, which was entertaining and irritating at the same time. I couldn't understand why anybody would want to be popular. "Hey, Elvis."

He walked alongside me. "Late for practice?"

We walked past one of the posters strewn around the school announcing plans for the new five-million-dollar science and technology wing. State-of-the-art computers, high-tech equipment, a forensics lab, all the good stuff. Lambert was scrambling for backers to fund it, and as with everything at Lambert, money was number one. "Yeah."

"You were in a meeting, weren't you? I heard Naomi Oxley talking about it."

I rolled my eyes. This place was gossip central, and I knew why Elvis was talking to me. "Maybe."

"With the grand pooh-bah, huh?"

I didn't answer.

His eyes brightened, and he took a skip. Elvis had been dying to be chosen for the Youth Leadership Group since he'd transferred here last year, because Elvis had spent his entire life trying to be included in things nobody would include him in. Sometimes he reminded me of a hamster on a wheel endlessly running to get somewhere he would never reach, and I didn't have the heart to tell him that the destination sucked. "Cool," he said. "What was it about?"

"You know the rules, Elvis. It's confidential."

"I know, I know, but you can tell me. I won't say anything. I promise." He looked around, smiling. "It's not like I *could* tell anybody, Jason. You're the only one who talks to me."

I sighed. The code of silence surrounding the Chamber of Five didn't mean a thing to me. I just didn't want to talk about it. Elvis would never be chosen for Youth Leadership because there was one unspoken stipulation. Money. He didn't have much.

There were two types of students at Joseph T. Lambert. One kind was preceded by truckloads of cash or status, and the other was Elvis: truly brilliant to the point of freakish dysfunction, and admitted for the reason the school had begun seventy years ago. He was gifted. You were either gifted at Lambert, or your parents gifted Lambert. Cut and dried.

"Did he say anything about me? You put my name in for the group when school started, and they haven't contacted me. Are they done choosing?"

When the Chamber chose new members for Youth Leadership, it was done in private. There were no announcements. "I don't know, and no, he didn't say anything about you."

"But—"

"Elvis, I don't know. I'm not in charge of how any of that works, okay?"

He deflated as we walked. "He chose you for the Chamber of Five, didn't he? Michael Paulson was the fifth member, but since he's graduated, they're short one." He glanced at me. "You're it, aren't you?"

I was, but I didn't want to tell him. My decision. My belief. My awe-inspiring rugged individualism and courage to stand up for what I knew was right for me. I could give him a five-minute oration on why I'd been chosen, but it would be five minutes of polished spin and outright lies.

The only reason I was at Joseph T. Lambert in the first place was because my dad bought my way in. *Grooming you for the future, son.* I could still hear his words, but I wasn't gifted. Good grades, sure. Anything other than average? Ha. "Why do you want to be in the Group so bad, Elvis? It's boring. And besides, you're a math genius, not a future politician."

"It's more than that."

I rolled my eyes. "Life isn't a popularity contest, Elvis."

"Do you know what the Pilkney Foundation is?"

"No."

"The top two percent of all math students in the country go there, and I've got a chance at making it. They have the best and most radical quantum physics program in the world. Full scholarship if I'm accepted into the foundation."

I swallowed, regretting my words and suddenly feeling like an absolute nothing next to this social outcast. "Wow."

He nodded. "There's only been three students from Lambert accepted to Pilkney in the last twenty-two years. All three were members of the Group."

"No kidding?"

"No kidding. Statistically speaking, my odds skyrocket."

"There's only thirty-three members of the Group."

"They've all been chosen?"

"I don't know. I didn't pay attention at the last meeting."

"Would you put a word in for me again? Please?"

"Sure." I glanced at my watch. "Listen, I'm late, and tryouts for the team start today. I'll talk to Carter."

CHAPTER TWO

As I SUITED up for tennis, I thought about Elvis. I reasoned that if any kind of good could come from being a member of the Chamber, it would be to help him. Maybe even others like him. It just sucked that I didn't want to be a part of it. If my father knew I had no intention of following him into politics, he'd take the congressional pin from his lapel and kill me with it.

My mother once told me I'd inherited her family genes. She wasn't born into royalty, though she was honest enough to say she liked the benefits of marrying into power. And though she was a trophy wife, the older I got, I realized that she was a trophy wife with a well-kept secret. She had a brain. I just couldn't figure out why she didn't use it.

Coach Yount called for pairs on the court for tryouts, but my usual partner from last year, Pauly Olson, was out with the flu. His father had picked it up in France the week before, and Pauly had been puking his guts out in French for the last two days. Parisian flu was classy, he'd told me on the phone. When you puked, you did it with flair.

As the team split off in pairs, choosing courts within the ivy-laced fence, the last guy left besides me was a freshman: a knobby-kneed rail of a kid with big ears, big feet, and a body that was too small for either. Not short, not tall, and all of fifteen years old to my seventeen. I groaned. I'd bet my bottom dollar the kid had never even hit a tennis ball.

I knew I'd make the team because I'd been one of the best for the last two years, and my uniform said so; the ranking on my sleeve showed it to everybody. Everything at Lambert had rankings. They lived on rankings. Status was everything.

I'd seen Big-ears around, and the word was he didn't talk. The silent type, keeps to himself. Fresh meat for Lambert. As I looked at him, dressed in cheap sweats, a wrinkled Lambert Physical Fitness T-shirt, and Payless tennis shoes, and holding an old racket, I almost felt sorry for him. Newbies tried out in the lowly and generic Lambert shirt; no official tennis uniform until you made the team.

As I looked him up and down, he kept his eyes on my face. He wasn't here because of his parents' money, that was for sure. I was tempted to ask him what made him a brilliant freak of nature, but I figured I'd get some sort of scientific equation instead of English. "Come on," I said, gesturing to our side of the court.

He followed, and as we took the court, he didn't know where to stand. I sighed. We'd be eaten alive. "Over there." I pointed with my racket. He moved. "Closer to the net. Three steps." He moved again. "There."

9

I looked across the court, and unfortunately, Hayden Kennedy stood there, a wicked smile on his face. Hayden Kennedy was in the Chamber of Five, the five that I'd joined less than twenty minutes ago. His father was a huge lobbyist, and just like his dad, he was nothing but a big polished turd with a mouth. He bounced a ball, laughing. "Got yourself a new pet, Weatherby?"

"Serve the ball, Kennedy." I readied myself. I'd be returning the serve, and Kennedy, despite being a complete smart-ass, was an ace on the court.

In another moment, Kennedy tossed the ball and smashed the hell out of it. It sped straight toward the new kid at almost eighty miles an hour, and just as he flinched to get out of the way, the ball nailed him square on the chest. The thud echoed over the other courts, the kid doubled over, and I shook my head in disgust. Leave it to Kennedy to pull something like that on a frosh.

As the yellow projectile bounced its way to a slow stop, Kennedy smiled at me from across the court, calling to the kid, "Sorry about that. Little bit rusty."

I shook my head as the newbie straightened. It had to have hurt. It couldn't not hurt. He'd have a bruise for weeks. "You okay?" I said. He went to the ball, bent, picked it up, and tapped it back to Kennedy. The kid didn't look at me. I called to him again.

He gripped his racket, staring over the net.

"You okay?"

He readied himself.

Kennedy guffawed. "Maybe he's deaf, Weatherby. You'd think with those radar dishes bolted to the side of his head he could pick up transmissions from Mars, but who knows, huh?"

I got in position as Kennedy bounced the ball. "Play it right, Kennedy. Don't be a dick."

"Sure, Weatherby. Sure. Sometimes I forget I live for making you happy."

So we played. The kid sucked so bad it wasn't funny, and halfway through the tryout, he excused himself to go to the restroom. Probably to slit his wrists. It was painful. It was so bad that Kennedy, the guy who never stops tormenting people, stopped taunting him when he got back. He just continually drilled the kid.

The kid didn't return a serve. He didn't say a word as I positioned him correctly, giving him hints and tips. He missed ball after ball, and when Coach Yount finally made his way to our court to observe and score, it took him all of five minutes to make four checks on his clipboard, shake his head, and move on.

The kid had an icicle's chance in hell of making the team, and I wondered what kind of self-hate had brought him on the court in the first place.

By the end of tryouts, I'd whipped up enough on Kennedy to get his mouth going again, which made me happy. Coach blew his whistle, and as we filed through the chain-link gateway to the gymnasium, the kid fell in line beside Kennedy, and of course Kennedy, at least five inches taller, bumped him aside with his shoulder and took his place.

Freshmen coming into Lambert were schooled quickly and efficiently on how things worked. Upperclassmen were everything; freshmen were nothing. Freshmen did what they were told, especially by Leadership Group members. The Chamber of Five were untouchable, and if you dared touch them, they ground you to dust.

As we filed into the locker room, I noticed the kid changing quickly, not bothering with a shower, and splitting before anybody else. I could almost feel the shame burning in him. Then Kennedy bellowed, his voice echoing from the walls, "WHO DID IT!?!"

I looked down the aisle of lockers. Kennedy was holding up his white dress shirt by the hanger. It was wet. It was yellow. I would have smiled if it didn't mean that somebody would die, and even though Kennedy had enough ex-freshmen enemies to last a lifetime, I knew who did it. Big-ears. Kennedy, after a moment of sluggish thought, knew, too.

As I hung my tennis shirt on the hanger and grabbed my bag, I wondered what the kid's deal was. He had to know Kennedy would be gunning for him. Maybe he was emo in disguise, death wish in hand. He was dead meat.

CHAPTER THREE

CARTER LOGAN SAT in a high-backed chair, one of five around the circular and deep-colored mahogany antique table set in the center of the Chamber. Next to him sat Hayden Kennedy, and two more guys, Michael Woodside and Steven Lotus, filled the chairs next to him. One remained empty. I stood at the door, which was adjacent to the study hall we'd met in the day before.

The Chamber was located in the main building on the third floor. The building was basically an ornate and hollow box ringed with three balconied floors of spacious rooms, including library, study hall, and administrative offices, and the Chamber was set directly opposite the main entrance down below. Often enough, you would see the five members standing at the railing outside the Chamber doors, looking down on the peasants scurrying through the indoor courtyard.

Only the five could enter the room without an invitation.

13

There was a lock on the door, and only five keys. The Chamber was off-limits.

Carter smiled, waving to me. "Welcome, Jason. Come over."

I walked in, nodding to each as he stood and shook my hand. All except Kennedy. He smirked at me, still pissed about tennis the day before, sure that I'd put the kid up to it somehow. He'd had to wear his tennis uniform around for the rest of the day due to his pissed-on shirt, and I'd cracked up every time I'd seen him.

Carter rolled his eyes. "Protocol is the foundation of civilization, Hayden. We're in the Chamber."

Kennedy grunted, standing and shaking my hand. He sat. I did, too. Carter nodded. "Welcome to your first meeting of the five. Jason, I'd like to extend you the chalice." With that, he reached for the goblet at the center of the table and slid it to me. "Drink."

I looked around, then at the contents of the cup. Dark red liquid. "What is it?"

Carter smiled. "The first tenet of the Chamber is trust, Jason. Implicit and total trust. You are amongst brothers now."

I took a breath, putting the goblet to my lips and sipping. Relief flooded through me. I was safe unless pig blood tasted like cherry Kool-Aid. After swallowing, I slid the goblet to Michael, who took a sip. As it was passed around, I looked at the wood-paneled Chamber. Antique globes, weathered and ancient maps, a marble chess set, framed copies of the United States Constitution and Bill of Rights, several pictures of past presidents, and other artifacts dotted the well-furnished room.

Carter rested his hands on the table after he'd taken a drink. He stared at the goblet in the center of the table. "*Novus ordo seclorum.* Do you know what that is, Jason?"

"No."

He pulled out a dollar bill, handing it to me. "Read the back, under the pyramid."

I did, and saw the words: NOVUS ORDO SECLORUM. "What does it mean?"

Carter smiled. "The translation is *A new order of the ages.*"

I frowned. "What does it mean?"

Carter nodded. "It means that our forefathers created a new order of power in the world. A power that would cover the globe. A power that we are a part of."

With that, Carter nodded to Kennedy, and Kennedy rose, walking to a desk in the corner of the Chamber. He brought back a black briefcase, setting it in front of Carter. As Carter turned the wheels of its combination lock, he spoke. "The Youth Leadership Group began over fifty years ago, and the Chamber of Five forty years ago. That man"— Carter pointed to a framed portrait on the wall—"was the founder."

He opened the briefcase. "The country was at war with itself over the Vietnam conflict, and the government was losing its power base to the hippies, freaks, dopeheads, and general do-nothing-for-something scum. A power base that had stood the test of time, but was eroding. The common people, simply put, were caught up in a cultural revolution that spelled out doom for the United States if it continued." He pointed to the picture again. "Senator Logan approached thirteen of the best private high schools in the country, this being one of them, and orchestrated the group to groom us for leadership. We are but one of thirteen groups, and the Chamber of Five is actually a chamber of sixty-five. There are lines of power in this country, Jason, and we're a part of it."

I looked at the picture. "Senator Logan?"

Carter smiled. "Yes. My grandfather."

I looked around the table. "Lines of power?"

"Yes. What do you think would happen if the majority of leaders in this country did not share a common view of power?"

I shook my head. "They don't. That's why we have political parties. We debate."

He chuckled. "We debate, yes, Jason, but what we debate is not important. *Who wins* is, and both Democrats and Republicans make sure who that winner is."

"Who wins, then?"

"*Novus ordo seclorum,* Jason. Republican or Democrat, it doesn't matter. Sure, they trifle with small issues that consume the people, but party lines only matter to the man blinded by idealism, and the American people, for their own good, are blinded by the charade of politics."

"Then tell me what the new order of the ages is."

Carter steepled his hands. "Money. Money equals power, and power equals control, Jason, and our government makes sure it stays in the right hands. Did you know that only men who owned land could vote when our country came into being? A small percentage of the population controlled our 'republic' until the law was changed, and it's been a struggle ever since. Our forefathers knew that to give power to the man with nothing would be the beginning of the end for America. Daily politics simply keeps the people focused on themselves." He paused. "The lines of power must be maintained, and we are the inheritors of that power, for the good of those who don't know any better. It's why we exist. It's why you were chosen."

"Because of my father?"

He nodded. "Not just your father, but this." With that, he took a file from the briefcase. My file. He opened it, sliding three sheets of paper toward me. "That is your personality profile. You remember filling it out?"

I stared at it, remembering. My father had stood over my shoulder while I answered the questions, correcting me, telling me what would look the best. I could almost feel his shadow over me right now. "Yes, I remember," I said, looking away. That profile was pure fiction; what my dad wanted me to be like, not what I was.

Carter nodded. "You are a born leader. Born into the blood of leadership. Just like all of us, and to one degree or another, the entire history of the Group. So welcome, Mr. Weatherby, and congratulations. You are a part of something tremendous."

With that, those around the table clapped their hands, and Carter, with a smile, nodded, taking out another file. "Now, on to business. We have a new member, and in accordance with the laws of the Chamber, a sacrifice must be made."

The others nodded. Kennedy smirked. I didn't understand.

Carter smiled. "You look confused, Jason. Let me explain. When a new member of the Chamber is chosen, the tenets of the order must be proven. The first, as I've said, is trust. The second is sacrifice."

The Kool-Aid came to mind. "What, you kill pigs or something?"

He laughed. "Of course not. This isn't a cult, though procession and tradition are important for any organization. Sacrifice and leadership go hand in hand, Jason, and the lines of power

17

need to be maintained in our favor. That takes sacrifice, because sacrifice proves trust."

I pointed to the file. "What's that about?"

"It's a file. A student file. It's also a test for you. To prove you are a true leader. To prove that you are willing to sacrifice for the good of all."

"What am I supposed to do with it?"

Carter leaned back, his head against the chair, his hands under his chin. "The student in that file does not belong here. It is your duty to . . . show him he doesn't belong here."

I glanced at the file, not opening it. "So I'm supposed to get this kid kicked out?"

He nodded.

"Just because he doesn't fit in? Why? Because he's smart?"

"No. We need brilliance."

I slid the file back. "Why doesn't he fit in?"

He shook his head. "You're not understanding, Jason. He doesn't matter. You do. And you have to prove your belief through trust and sacrifice, just like with anything else. Each person at this table, including me, was given a task to show his determination and ability to lead."

I squirmed. "I'm not doing it."

Carter smiled. "Sacrifice goes both ways, Jason. Even a simple soldier in our simple army needs to sacrifice to be accepted, no? He has to prove he's worthy. This is no different. Leadership is the ability to make decisions for the good of all, and Lambert, for the good of all, needs to be kept clean. Our status is important, your future here is important, and you must show us. Though the student chosen for termination is smart, he has an extensive juvenile criminal record. He does not belong here."

18

"This is bullshit."

He studied me. "I would have expected understanding. Hasn't your father ever grappled with decisions that may hurt a few but that benefit the majority? He's a great man."

I swallowed. "It's not right."

"Then perhaps this file"—he pointed to mine—"should be replaced with that file." He pointed to the file I'd turned away. "Would that be good, Jason? Would your father be happy about his son being expelled from Joseph T. Lambert School for the Gifted? My God"—he rolled his eyes to the ceiling—"it would probably make the papers if it was bad enough."

"You're crazy."

He laughed softly, glancing at the other members. His eyes came back to me. "Do you recall Mark Spencer from last year?"

"Yeah. He trashed Professor Downey's math class."

Carter sat back. "No he didn't. Kennedy here did." He studied a fingernail, absently picking. "I hear Mark is out of juvenile detention now. Isn't he, Kennedy?"

Kennedy nodded, his goofy smile broad. "Yeah. His dad sent him to some private school in Idaho for fuckups," he snickered. "Land of potatoes."

Carter leaned forward. "See, Jason, there's things at work here beyond your control. That's why we need lines of power. Trust. Sacrifice. We're a brotherhood." He gestured to the files. "This is a proving ground, Jason, and you must prove yourself."

"Don't threaten me, Carter."

He smiled. "It's not a threat, Jason. It's an invitation to your future." He paused. "Every Chamber member since the beginning has had to prove himself. It's like being in the Boy Scouts. You have to earn your Merit Badge, be initiated." He eyed me.

"I don't want to see you caught up on the wrong side of winning. You don't, either."

"It's not fair."

His eyes lit, intense. "Fair has nothing to do with life, and that's what this is about. Those who believe in fair are the ones who lose." He leaned forward, clasping his hands on the table. "Only the strongest can sacrifice the weak, because only the strongest can see what's best for everybody. It's our job, and we'd have chaos otherwise." He eyed me. "I'm surprised that with your background, you'd be so ignorant."

I stared at him, my insides squirming.

He leaned back. "I know this is difficult. It always is the first time, and I understand that. You're a good person. We all are. But we have choices to make, and those choices can hurt sometimes." He pointed to the file. "Bring that with you and think about it. Take some time." His eyes glinted. "And by the way, I already sent your father a letter of congratulations about your acceptance to the Chamber."

I looked at the file, not appreciating one bit the leverage of the letter. Carter knew how to play the game, and I was stuck. I took the file. "I do need to think about it."

He studied me, a small smile on his face as he nodded. "I want to show you something before we adjourn. An example of sacrifice to prove trust." He spoke to the Chamber. "We have a guest today. Michael, open the door. Our visitor should be waiting."

As Michael rose, Carter's eyes met mine, and the corners of his mouth turned up. Then he winked. Michael opened the door, and a girl, her hands clasped, stepped in, ducking her head timidly and looking around. She was pretty, and I recognized her from history class last year. Carter stood, welcoming her. "Come in, Brooke. Come in."

She walked across the room, stopping a few feet from the table. Michael took his seat. Carter sat down, speaking to her. "Thank you for coming."

She swallowed, standing uncomfortably in the silent room. "Thank you for having me."

Carter nodded. "And how is your mother?"

She smiled. "Fine. She's just made partner at the law firm, and she has an eye on becoming a federal judge."

Carter gazed at us. "Brooke's mother is an attorney in the city. She represents congressmen and senators who find themselves bogged down with the intricacies of leadership. In fact, she represented Congressman Hinks this last year concerning his . . . difficulties with monogamy." He smiled. "You know, Brooke, Mr. Weatherby here has a father in Congress."

She smiled again, looking at me. Pretty eyes. Brown and soft, like a fawn doe. "Yes, I know."

Carter cleared his throat. "Well, to the business at hand. I received your mother's letter of recommendation for your election to the Leadership Group, and I was very impressed."

Her eyes brightened. "Thank you."

"Hoping to attend Harvard, yes?"

She nodded. "Yes. I'm following in my mother's footsteps."

He sat back. "Wonderful. Then you'll be happy to know you've been accepted into the Group. Congratulations."

She grinned, nodding. Relief spread over her face. "Thank you so much. You don't know—"

Carter held up his hand, stopping her. "However, there is

one last thing. The Group is here for you, Brooke. You and your future. The service it does for you will carry on far beyond this school, and you will no doubt be accepted to Harvard with the help of our backing."

She beamed. "Thank you."

Carter nodded. "As the Group serves you, you must serve the Group. We all have responsibilities, and occasionally those responsibilities may test us." He glanced at me. "Isn't that right, Jason?"

Silence.

Carter went on. "You understand this, Brooke?"

"Yes."

He nodded again with finality. "Good. I knew you'd understand. Sometimes what we want must be sacrificed for what is best."

She grimaced, a look of uncertainty on her face. "Well, I suppose so."

Carter studied her. "You sound unsure, Brooke. Do you believe your mother enjoyed representing a man who cheated on his wife with a seventeen-year-old congressional page?"

She shook her head. "No. She didn't like him at all. He was a creep."

Carter smiled. "Of course she didn't like him. She represented him because she knows what is best. Best for her and best for this country. The good Congressman Hinks does far outweighs the bad, and your mother sacrificed a part of herself because she understands this. We all must do these things."

She nodded. "That's what she told me."

He ran his finger along the ridge of his jaw. "So you do understand."

22

"Yes."

A moment passed, then Carter slid me a glance. His voice floated softly across the room. "Unbutton your blouse, Brooke."

I held my breath. No way. This wasn't happening. Brooke stood with her eyes at her feet. Carter smiled. "Your mother will be so proud, Brooke. Imagine how happy she'll be. Imagine Harvard."

A full minute passed, silence in the Chamber. I met Carter's eyes, and he shook his head, putting his fingers to his lips. Brooke unbuttoned the first button. Then the second. After another moment and with her eyes still on her feet, she'd opened the last one. Carter, his voice soft, spoke. "Take your blouse off, Brooke."

I sat, transfixed, unable to do anything. I couldn't believe this was happening. I couldn't believe it was happening for my benefit. Carter Logan was showing me his power, and I couldn't even breathe. My dad's angry image flashed through my mind.

She sighed, her breath quivering, then did it. Her bare shoulders, pale and soft and defined, trembled.

"Fantastic. Now your bra."

She hesitated, then unclasped it, letting it fall to the floor. Her breasts were full and firm. My stomach squirmed and my mind revolted against what was happening. Sickness spread through me, but I did nothing. There was a detachment. There had to be, because between my father and this school and Carter Logan, I was powerless.

Silence hammered the room like the blood pounding in my ears, and Brooke stood like a statue, her chin down, hands clasped in front of her.

Carter studied our faces one by one. Then he smiled. "That

is all. Dismissed, Brooke. And congratulations. I will be writing your mother a letter of membership. You'll be a fantastic addition to the Group. Thank you."

Immediately Brooke covered herself, and as she turned to leave, her eyes met mine. Pure humiliation filled them. As the door closed, Carter thrust his chin up, resting his head against the chair. "She'll make a fine member."

Chuckles.

Carter lowered his chin. "What did we just see, gentlemen?"

More chuckles. Steven spoke, laughing. "A whore?"

Carter turned to him. "You think so? Do you think we just saw a private little sex show from some floozy?"

Steven swallowed. "Well, she showed us her boobs. . . ."

"Stand up."

Steven took a breath, then pushed his chair back and stood.

Carter looked at me. "Did you see a whore, Jason?"

"No. I saw you take advantage of her."

Carter's face was a rock. "What we saw was power, gentlemen. Not my power, though. What we witnessed was the power of what a person wants as opposed to what a person *needs*. She's a good girl. A fine girl. A girl with expectations, and a girl who *understands*." His eyes bored into me.

Steven, still standing, smirked. "A good girl? Then why . . ."

Carter's face hardened. "Are you a whore, Steven?"

"Of course not. I'm . . ."

Carter's jaw muscles worked under the delicate cheekbones of his face, his anger clear. "Unbutton your shirt."

Steven stared.

Carter shrugged, meeting Steven's eyes. "Make your decision, Steven. Now."

Silence, then slowly Steven unbuttoned his shirt.

"Take it off."

Steven took it off, his pudgy midsection reminding me of a frosted donut hole.

Carter went on. "Are you a whore now? Are you not standing in this Chamber just as Brooke did, and did you not call her a whore?"

He took a deep breath, his face flushed, his eyes straight ahead, staring at nothing. "Yes."

Carter grinned. "Good. Now you see." His eyes roamed the table, then landed on me. "We're all whores in the idiotic and shallow way Steven sees life. Every one of us is. Every living human being has a price, and it's just a matter of what we are willing to do to get what we need." He looked at Steven. "Do you understand, Steven? Do you understand that you're as much of a whore as Brooke is?"

"Yes."

Carter nodded, all the while his eyes riveted on me. "Good. Then put your clothes on and get out of my sight."

CHAPTER FOUR

"I RECEIVED A LETTER from the president of the Chamber. Carter Logan? I know his father. You were a shoo-in for it, son."

I looked at Dad through the bathroom mirror as I combed my hair. "Thanks."

He nodded, standing at the door. "I had a staffer forward it to a dean at Stanford. I've spoken to him previously about you, and he's impressed."

"My grades aren't good enough for Stanford."

He smiled. "You're a Weatherby. That's enough. But it doesn't mean you get a free ride." His smile disappeared. "I've put a lot on the line for your education, Jason. Don't screw it up. Get the grades."

"Sure," I said.

"Good, because if you don't, I'm sending you to military school in Vermont. I've already told your mother I'm not paying

Lambert this much money unless you begin to respect the opportunity you've been given. Last year almost broke the camel's back, and I'm not putting up with it this year. I will not have a misfit for a son, and I will not risk your making me the laughing-stock on the Hill." He paused. "Straight and narrow, Jason. Straight and narrow."

"Yeah."

He studied me, tightening his belt. "Your tie isn't straight."

I adjusted my tie, and he stood behind me, inspecting my suit. His neck flushed. "The jacket cuffs are short," he grumbled, then poked his head out my bathroom door and yelled down the hall, "Tiff! Tiffany!"

Mom came bustling down the hall, her heels echoing on the hardwood. "We're going to be late. The driver is outside." She poked her head in the bathroom, smiling when she saw me. "You look wonderful, Jason. Wonderful."

My dad shook his head. "His sleeves are short."

She studied them, frowning, then smiled. "I'll take him to the tailor next week. He's growing."

My dad looked at himself in the mirror, slicking his hair back and inspecting his teeth. "I'm going to one of the biggest fund-raisers of the year and my son looks like he picked his jacket off a rack at Goodwill. Great."

"I'm sorry, honey. I said I'll take him." She smiled again. "Jason, you look just fine. Nobody will notice."

I shrugged. "I'm fine with it."

Dad rinsed his hands and dried them, throwing the towel on the counter. "Of course you're fine with it because you don't have any standards." He faced me, tension flushing his face.

"You're seventeen years old, Jason. You should have known your suit didn't fit, you should have taken care of the problem, and I shouldn't be standing here dealing with you saying you're fine with it. It's not fine. You're not fine. You look like a clown."

Silence. I looked at myself in the mirror. "More like a monkey on a leash, I'd say."

He jabbed a finger at me through the mirror. "Don't start with me," he said, then turned to leave the bathroom.

I shrugged. "Just a difference of opinion is all. I'd say I look sort of like you, Dad."

He swung around, and Mom's face tightened. She looked down. "Jason, please."

His eyes blazed into me. "No, Tiff. I want to hear why our son, with that smart-ass mouth, thinks he even deserves to have an opinion in this house."

"I'm not allowed to have an opinion now? Before, it was just saying mine were idiotic and stupid, but now it looks like I don't even get to have one."

He looked away for a moment, shook his head, and spoke. "You don't 'get' anything in this world. You earn it." Then he turned and walked out, bellowing to both of us to get in the god-damned car.

The Lidgerwood Country Club sprawled across the manicured grounds like a paparazzi photo on the front page of a gossip rag. Valet attendants hustled back and forth, helping women from cars, directing limos to parking areas, bobbing their heads and smiling for tips. Just the way it should be to make important people feel important.

I opened my door to the twinkle lights strung through the

trees, and my father put his hand on my knee. "You don't get out by yourself."

After the near explosion in the bathroom, I knew I was pushing my luck. I shut the door, waiting for the attendant.

As we were escorted into the club, Mom and Dad stopped to jabber with another couple, and I found my way in, handing my overcoat to the coat-check girl and walking over the marble floor inlaid with the crest of the club, which was two old-fashioned golfer guys staring up at a flying eagle. To the right was the club restaurant, which I'd been to a million times, and across from that was the bar, where my dad had been a million times. He'd made more money in that place than in his office.

Farther on and past the golf shop, several conference rooms, and the restrooms, I took a left and headed down toward the banquet hall, where the shindig was heating up.

"Hey."

I turned, and Michael Woodside, from the Chamber of Five, sauntered toward me. I shook his hand. "Hey, Woodsie."

He stopped, looking around and sliding his hands into his slacks pockets. He was taller than me, played lacrosse for the school team, and had perfectly white, straight teeth. His father was a heart surgeon, and was also the chairman of some national medical association. He flew to Washington every month to meet with the president.

"Figured you'd be here."

I glanced around at the milling people. "Yep."

He looked me up and down. "Your jacket sleeves are too short."

"I'm aware of that."

He chuckled. "Got a ration of shit from your dad, I bet."

"Yeah."

He shook his head. "My dad had a case of diarrhea mouth once when I had a scuff on my shoe. The guy is obsessive."

I looked around. Couples and small groups of socialites passed by us, and we stood, uncomfortable with knowing each other but not knowing each other. Then Michael smiled. I turned, and Kennedy walked toward us and shook Michael's hand. "Hello, men." He glanced over his shoulder, then turned back and grinned. "Did you see who is here, and who is right now heading this way?"

We turned, and the girl Brooke was coming down the hall with her mother. My stomach sank. Kennedy spoke under his breath before they neared. "You know her mother, Woodsie. Make it good."

Brooke avoided eye contact as they passed, but of course, her mother gave a huge smile and dragged her over. "Well, hello, Michael. How are you?" She looked him up and down. "It's been over a year since we last met. You look sharp. Very sharp."

Woodsie smiled, shaking her hand. "Thank you, ma'am. It's nice to see you."

Brooke stood back, looking away. She wore a peach-colored dress that accentuated her hips, and I had a hard time not staring. With her hair done up, she looked beautiful, her slender neck graceful, her eyes dark and anxious. I couldn't help thinking about what I'd seen that day as my eyes involuntarily roamed to her chest. Her mother looked at Kennedy and me. "Brooke? These must be classmates, too?" She pulled her daughter forward. "Perhaps introductions are in order?"

Brooke hesitated. I stepped up. "Jason Weatherby, ma'am. It's nice to meet you."

She shook my hand and nodded. "Yes. Your father is Congressman Weatherby."

I smiled. "Only on Mondays, Wednesdays, and Fridays, ma'am. The rest of the time he's telling me what to do."

She laughed, thinking it was a joke, and looked to Kennedy. He stepped forward, shaking her hand. "Hayden Kennedy, Mrs. Naples. A pleasure to meet you." He nodded. "We . . ." He glanced at Brooke. "Saw your daughter today." He grinned. "And congratulations on the Group membership. She's got a fantastic-looking résumé. Stellar, actually. In fact, everybody in the room took a close look at it." He beamed. "Very well put together."

Mrs. Naples blushed, flattered. If I could have punched Kennedy in the face, I would have. Brooke cringed, and tears welled in her eyes. I cleared my throat. "It was nice meeting you, Mrs. Naples. Have a good night."

She gave me a stern glance, apparently put off that I'd put her off, and after a moment, they left. I turned to Kennedy. "You are the biggest asshole in the world, Kennedy."

He laughed. "Better an asshole than a comedian. Only on Mondays, Wednesdays, and Fridays? Brilliant, Weatherby. Almost peed my pants it was so funny."

"Go to hell. That was uncool."

He grinned. "By the way, how's your pet? He doing well?"

"What?"

"The kid. You know, tennis. The guy I drilled the other day." He turned to Woodsie. "What's his name? Dipshit Dingledork? Was that it?"

"Thomas Singletary. He lives in the Heights."

"Yeah. Poor boy Tom from the slums." Kennedy looked at me. "Doesn't his mom check out groceries at Walmart, Weatherby?

The one in Lincoln Heights? Or does she sell herself to pay Tom's tuition?"

I looked at him. "I have no idea."

Kennedy smirked. "You don't? You should."

I sighed, tired of him, but completely confused about what this conversation was about. "Why?"

He waggled his finger at me. "Because . . . ," he said, turning to leave, "he's the one in your file, and the games are about to begin."

It clicked then, and all the pieces fell together. "That's not cool, Kennedy. I've got to kick him out because he pissed on your uniform?"

He smiled. "I'd like it to be, but no. Carter had him picked out before it happened." Then he was gone, a big and rich galoot flopping his feet down the hall.

I deflated. "Bastard."

Woodsie nodded. "Can't say I like him too much, either. More irritating than dangerous, though."

I looked at him. "You did it, didn't you?"

"What?"

"The file initiation. You were given one when you were chosen."

He nodded again. "Carter is right, Jason. I don't like it, but—"

"But what? He's not right. He's an ass. And a psycho, as far as I'm concerned."

He shrugged. "You've never met his father, have you?"

"No."

"His grandfather may have been a senator, but his dad is nothing but a washed-up drunk of a judge. The embarrassment of the family. He ran for governor three times in the last eighteen years and lost every time, and he was suspended from the bench last year for drunk driving. Barely made it to the federal bench before they kicked his ass out. I met him once at a banquet, and by the end of it, he was stumbling around making a fool of himself. Goes after every piece of tail he can put his hands on, too. Carter had to carry him out. He hates him."

"Pity party for Carter."

Woodsie shrugged. "He's right about the money. My dad paid big bucks just to get my application into the school, Jason. And the tuition sets him back at least a new Seven Series BMW every year. He told me if I fuck this up, I'm out. Out of the house, out of the family, no trust fund when I turn twenty-one, and no college." He paused. "So I do what I have to do."

"Sucks for you."

"Carter is right about a lot, Jason. We do what we need to do, but that doesn't mean I like it. Brooke is nice. I've known her for seven years."

"Who decides what happens? Carter?"

He lowered his voice. "You think Carter is the one controlling the rules? He might decide *who*, but he doesn't decide what."

I nodded. "Like with this Singletary kid. Kennedy had a beef with him, and now I'm the payback on it. It's bull."

"That might be true, but there's more."

"What, then?"

He leaned close, almost whispering. "Where do you think he got those files? Where do you think they came from? Think he stole them from the chancellor's office? They either ignore it politely, or quietly make it happen because they know who funds the school. The Chamber is powerful, Jason. And you know as well as I do that tradition is strong. Sometimes stronger than right and wrong."

"I don't know . . . I just—"

He stopped me. "You do know, man. Just like I do. There's a reason for everything that ever happens at that school, and I'm telling you right now that if you don't do what the Chamber wants, you'll be out. And Carter will be the one who makes sure it hurts, because the guy *likes* hurting people." He looked around. "You remember two years ago? Paul Thorburne?"

I did. A picture of Paul giving a guy a blow job had circulated through the school, and three days later, he was gone. His father had been president of the American Association of Evangelical Pastors. *Had been* being the key words. The story of the antigay leader's son who was gay had been plastered all over the news for a solid week, and he resigned. I groaned. "Don't tell me . . ."

He nodded. "He wasn't even gay, Jason. Carter paid some guy to force him to do it, and the picture was taken. The guy put a gun to his head. A *gun*."

"Because he refused to take a file, right?"

Woodsie whistled under his breath. "Carter has a wicked midget in his head, man. I don't even know how he thinks some crap up."

I shrugged. "Paul could have just said it was a setup."

He screwed his eyes up at me. "Were you born yesterday? You know how things work. A guy says he was forced to give a blow job because he refused to do what a secret society told him? Yeah, sure. The Chamber doesn't even exist on paper, Jason. It's not even officially sanctioned by the school, even though everybody knows about it."

I looked at him, suddenly uncomfortable. "How do you know about Paul? Do you guys just sit in that room and shoot the shit about ruining lives?"

"No."

"Then how?"

He cleared his throat, hesitating. "Because I took the picture."

I stared at Woodsie for a moment, searching his eyes for any pleasure or humor, and I found none. Just shame found in a truth. And right then, I knew what I was up against.

An hour and a half later and after listening to a bunch of notables, including my father, blather on about how much they cared about cancer victims, I'd had enough. I stood, walking through the crowd and stepping into the hall. I wandered, stopping in front of the golf shop and staring blankly at a rack of shirts behind the glass. Then I saw her.

Peach. She walked toward the restrooms, and I hesitated. I knew she didn't want to see me. Or know me. "Brooke."

She stopped, turning, and when she saw me, she flinched. Then she turned around and hurried away.

I jogged down the hall. "Brooke, please. Stop."

She stopped, turning. The doe eyes weren't soft. "What?"

I studied her face. I didn't know what to do. I didn't know a thing to say to make her feel better, but I had to, and the seconds were ticking. "You look nice," I blurted.

She crossed her arms over her chest. "Another little joke from the little boys' club?"

I looked away. "No . . . I just, I didn't have anything to do with it."

Rage and humiliation flushed her face. "Sure, Jason. Sure. Here, you want to see more?" Then she grabbed the straps of her dress, sliding them from her shoulders. "Here, take a good look, you sick pervert."

I reached up and grabbed her hands, looking around. "Don't. Don't do that."

She stared at me, tears in her eyes. "Why not? That's all I am, right? A show for the boys?"

"Then report it. Do it. Tell the chancellor, and tell him I was there."

She clenched her teeth.

"You won't, will you?"

"I can't."

"I know. You can't report it for the same reason I had to sit there and watch it. But I didn't want to."

She put her hands on her hips. "Liar."

Anger welled in my chest. I took a breath. "Listen, I just wanted to apologize. That's all. I'm sorry it happened."

Her face tightened. "Apology not accepted." Then she turned on her heel.

"Brooke."

She turned. "What?"

"You could have walked out just as easily as me."

After that, she stared at me for a moment, rage and shame at the truth of what I'd said in her eyes, then turned and walked away.

CHAPTER FIVE

"SINGLETARY, THOMAS," Coach Yount called. "Cut." Then he moved on to the next name. Most of the freshmen were going down in flames.

Kennedy laughed under his breath, nudging me. "That was a no-brainer. The guy can play tennis like your mother has kids. Fucked up and retarded."

"Don't you ever get sick of hearing your own voice, Kennedy? I'd kill myself if I was you."

"I'm crying inside, Weatherby. You wound me."

"I'm sure I do."

He grinned. "Chamber meeting today at four. Be there or be an idiot."

I shuddered inside. The last two days had been spent agonizing over the kid and what I should do. I didn't like admitting it one bit, but Carter Logan scared me. He could hurt me, because he could hurt my father, and I was trapped.

I'd studied the kid's file, and it wasn't good. None of it. His father had been killed by a drunk driver two years ago; his mother checked out groceries at Walmart in the Heights, and her annual income was a little over twenty thousand dollars. My father spent twenty thousand last year on having the pool retiled.

As I read deeper into his file, I reached his academic reports. Elvis had nothing on this kid. He wasn't gifted in *a* subject; he was gifted in *every* subject. His IQ was off the charts, and as I read his test scores, I realized he wasn't some sort of idiot savant with a chance to find a niche somewhere; he was a kid walking around with more brainpower than entire countries. He'd scored in the top one percent in all subjects.

Then I got to his police record.

Three stints in juvie for aggravated assault, two misdemeanor theft charges (dismissed), vandalism, and one felony charge for tampering with an Internet server. Of all things, the tampering charge had to do with hacking into federal courthouse files. He was a hacker, and for how innocent the kid looked, he wasn't.

I couldn't do it, though. No matter how bad he was, he hadn't done anything to me. But I didn't see a way out of it. As we filed from the tennis courts, I fell in line beside him. I was fully a head taller than him. "Has Kennedy bugged you at all?"

He didn't answer.

"Don't talk much, huh?"

"Not to people at this school."

"Why are you here, then?"

"None of your business."

"He's got it out for you."

He gave nothing away, this small, skinny kid. No emotion. "I don't care."

"You should."

"I don't."

I stopped, grabbing his shoulder. "Do you not understand this? I'm trying to help you here, and you're being a prick about it. You're in trouble, Thomas. You shouldn't have pissed on his stuff."

He snapped his shoulder away. "Don't touch me."

The look in his eyes reminded me of his file. Aggravated assault. "I'm trying to give you a break."

His face finally broke, but it wasn't fear or anger or anything. It was a smile. A genuine and easy smile. "What makes you think I need help with anything?"

"What, you think you're tough or something? Kennedy *likes* pain."

His eyes met mine. The smile was still on his face, and his voice came soft. "Don't you have bigger problems to deal with?"

"Than what?" I shrugged. "You're the new frosh meat is all, and you're making things easier."

"For who?"

"Kennedy."

He looked away.

I shook my head. "Fine, man. I don't give a crap, anyway. I was just trying to do you a favor."

He laughed. "Want some advice, rich boy?"

"What?"

"Fuck off."

"So you're the poor kid in a school full of rich pricks. Too bad for you."

He shrugged. "Go make yourself feel good on somebody else."

"You're an ass, you know that? I didn't do anything to you."

He met my eyes, and there was no backing down in them. "Fine. Now that we're in agreement, maybe you should just go back to your little club, huh?"

"What club? The Chamber?"

He smiled again. "You enjoyed the show?"

I furrowed my brow, not understanding, but Brooke instantly came to mind. He couldn't know about that. Nobody could, unless one of us had talked. Carter came to mind, and I wondered what kind of game he was playing. "What show?"

"The tennis show."

I studied his face. He was like a book with no words in it. "Whatever. Eat shit, Singletary. You deserve what you get."

Lunch rolled around, and Elvis rolled around with it, bobbing his head and smiling like a big goof. He had a habit of avoiding the tile lines on the floor, which made walking with him feel like I was watching a guy play hopscotch. "Hey, Jason. Guess what?"

"What?"

He grinned, showing big teeth as he shortened a step to miss a line. "I got a meeting today."

"With who?"

He slapped me on the back. "You. The Chamber. Carter sent me a note. Today at four. And you know what? I think I'm being accepted."

"How's that?"

"Because the logical conclusion would be that, Jason. Why would they call me in, otherwise? Besides, the note congratulated me on being selected to appear before them. It said that I should thank you, too, so thank you."

My mind was on Thomas. "Cool."

"You'll be there?"

"I suppose so."

He smiled, clapping me on the shoulder. "To success, my friend. To success." Then he was gone, whistling down the hall, happy as a side-stepping, hopscotching clam.

I walked into the Chamber, and the five high-backed chairs were set up in a row, the table gone and an empty space in front. Kennedy, Woodsie, and Steven sat, and Carter was nowhere to be found. Woodsie nodded. "Weatherby."

"Hey, Woodsie." I nodded to Steven, who nodded back.

Kennedy smiled. "No greeting for me, brother?"

I smiled back, sitting. "Hello, asswipe."

Kennedy laughed. "I like you, Weatherby, but I like your mother better. Total MILF." He smiled again. "Are they natural?"

I ignored him. "Why are the chairs like this?"

Woodsie took a piece of gum from his pocket. "Interview today. Your buddy, I think."

Kennedy smirked. "That Presley guy? What is the world coming to? The guy is like the son of his brother's mother's sister or some freaky shit like that. You can tell a guy is inbred by the eyes. Close together and screwy."

I turned to Kennedy, squinting at him. "I know your family has money, but come on. It's like buying your dog into Lambert and expecting him to learn anything other than to lick his balls and shit in the backyard."

Kennedy guffawed. "That's why I like you, man. Sincerely. I do. But I'm a rich dog."

Woodsie laughed. "Goes to show you, Weatherby. You can beat the shit out of a dog, but you can't make the dog stop eating shit."

Kennedy rolled his eyes. "You think he won that verbal sparring match, Woods? I killed him. The inbred joke was way better than the lame dog thing."

Woodsie laughed again.

Kennedy shrugged. "Fine, then. We'll leave it to Steven." He looked to Steven. "All right, Lotus, who won? Me or pukehead?"

He took a breath. "I don't know."

Kennedy furrowed his brow. "Are you still all sensitive about the whore thing, Steve-o? Come on, we're all whores, just like Carter said. You're just better at it than most."

Steven sank into his chair, staring at the door.

Kennedy rolled his eyes again, slouching back into his seat. "I meant that in a good way, man. I did. In fact, you sort of turned me on when you had your shirt off. All tingly down under." He laughed, and just then Carter walked in, shutting the door behind him.

He held a file and whistled a nameless tune as he walked over. "Hello, brothers." Nods and handshakes, then Carter took his seat in the center of the row, beside me. "Business on the agenda today, men. An interview for the last spot in the Youth Leadership Group, but we've a decision to make before this interview takes place." He crossed his ankle over his knee and fiddled with his shoelace. "As you all know, the Lambert school elections will be held in two weeks for the general-population student council. . . ." He waved it off. "I know they're lame duck, but we can't allow the wrong people to take positions, particularly the student-body president, vice president, and treasurer. Of the six positions, we need at least four to own a majority vote on policy, particularly budget. I've already spoken to three Leadership Group members who will run, and of course we'll win, but as for the president, we need a member of the five in power to have absolute assurances. One of us." He looked at Steven. "You will be running for president."

Kennedy laughed. "What? The guy can't even tie his shoes without a maid, and you want him to be student-body president?"

Steven slumped further in his chair.

Carter nodded. "Steven will be perfect for the position, Kennedy." He looked over at him. "Would you prefer to run?"

Kennedy shrugged. "Well, yeah. At least, we'd have—"

Carter interrupted. "The Chamber can exert its will at this school, Kennedy, but only to a certain extent. I'm afraid you are too much of an asshole to win. Everybody hates you. Even with the Group backing you, we'd have to resort to violence, which I hate. Steven will be running."

I shook my head. "I thought you said we had to make the decision, Carter."

He smiled. "We did."

"No, you did. And not that I agree with Kennedy, but Steven doesn't exactly have the charisma needed." I looked at Steven. "Not bagging on you, Steve, but you don't seem too excited."

He shrugged. I was beginning to wonder if an intelligent conversation with the guy would consist of more than two words.

Carter smiled. "I'll take that as an affirmative shrug. Congratulations, Steven." He looked at the file on his lap. "Now, on to the interview."

I wouldn't back down. "What about Woodsie? He's a natural for it."

Carter frowned. "Steven will do an excellent job because he understands our mission."

I rolled my eyes. "In other words, he'll do what you tell him."

Carter raised his eyebrows, cocking an eye at me. "Very good, Jason. You're already getting the hang of things. Now, on to our guest." He took a file from a folder. "Mr. Presley." He looked up at me. "You happen to be friends with this student?"

I nodded. "He's got a chance at a prestigious program, and scholarship, if he makes it in. It's important."

Kennedy groaned. "An inbred Elvis impersonator."

Carter winked at me, tapping the file. "Actually, a very impressive record, and an absolute asset to the scientific community. Brilliant in math, right, Jason?"

"Yes."

Carter nodded at the file. "You recommended him, correct?"

"Yes."

A moment passed as we waited. He leaned toward me. "So have you thought about your assignment, Jason?"

"Still thinking."

His voice slid through the room smooth and easy. Comforting. "Very good. Some things need deliberation. I thought this interview would be appropriate to show you how the Chamber can work with you in the same way that you work with us."

I relaxed a bit, but I knew that with Carter, the first mistake

44

was to let your guard down. "Thanks. He is smart, and there's no way he could get in without the Chamber."

"That's what we're here for. To help each other."

Kennedy cut in. "Dude, have you seen the guy walk? I think he's got some disorder or something."

"He skips lines. It's a thing with him," I said.

Kennedy laughed. "Step on a crack, break your mother's back."

Carter laid his hands on the table. "Kennedy, are you finished showing everybody here what happens when the wrong people have children?"

Just then Elvis knocked on the door. Carter called out, "Enter."

The door opened, and Elvis, his hair combed for once, sharply parted, walked in. He'd pressed his slacks and wore his formal blazer, with a kerchief in the breast pocket. He nodded, closing the door behind him, and smiled. "Hi."

Carter gestured to him. "Welcome, Mr. Presley. Come in."

Elvis walked to the center of the room, looking around. "Should I get a chair?"

Carter studied the file. "You may stand."

"Sure."

Carter closed the file, looking up and smiling. He crossed his knee over his leg. "Membership in the Group is important to you, yes?"

"Yes. I've a chance at being accepted to the Pilkney Foundation for math and science. One of the most prestigious in the world." He smiled, his teeth huge and white. "It's hard to get in to."

Carter went on. "And what do you plan on doing once you've attended?"

He beamed. "Quantum physics, nanotechnology, and—"

Carter tapped a pen on the file. "Mr. Presley, what does your father think about it?"

He smiled wide. "He's happy that I have a chance to—"

"What does he do?" Carter looked at the file. "Oh, yes. He works for the parks department, right?"

"Yes, he does. For over twenty-five years."

"Wonderful. We need people like that. Gardeners and such. Does he carry around a trash bag and one of those poker things to pick up litter? I've seen them do that, you know, and I just hate people who litter. Especially in our nice parks." He paused. "We pay taxes for those things, and we pay men like your father to serve us. Did he go to trash-picking-up school?"

Elvis faltered. "Well, he . . ."

I clenched my teeth, leaning toward Carter. "That's enough, Carter."

He waved me off. "I'm sure he's a good little worker, Mr. Presley. Does he wear a uniform? Like a janitor? With the keys jangling on his belt? When I was a child, I was fascinated by those men. I'd drop things just to watch them pick it up."

A sheen of sweat glowed on Elvis's forehead, and his eyes flicked to me. "I . . . he is very supportive of me. Yes. He is."

Carter chuckled. "No worries here, Mr. Presley. I can see you are ashamed of him, and I understand. It's not your fault, is it? It's just fascinating to me that here you are, at this school, and your father is picking up other people's trash for a living. That is America at its best, yes?" He stared at Elvis. "My dad used to give our caretaker a turkey at Christmas for doing such a good job. Does your father get turkeys?" Carter looked around. "Maybe we should send him a turkey. Yes. Let's send him a turkey for doing such a good job. My father always taught me that a simple man likes simple things."

Elvis sniffed, blinking, his eyes on Carter. "I'm sorry, but what does my father have to do with . . ." He glanced at me, then back to Carter. "Carter, I thought I was coming here to—"

Carter snapped, quick and vicious, "Call me sir."

Elvis looked down. "Sir."

I stood. "Knock it off, Carter."

Carter smiled, ignoring me. "Mr. Presley, you are a freak. A bizarre, genetic malfunction, and I can't understand for the life of me what made you think that you could ever, ever be in the Youth Leadership Group." He folded his hands on his lap. "Application denied. Get out."

Elvis looked up, his face wracked and broken, like he'd been flayed alive for something he didn't understand. "But the note said . . ."

I turned to Elvis. "Get out, Elvis. Right now."

He stood still.

"GO!" I barked. He left. I turned to Carter, grabbing his shirt and smashing him into the chair. "I should beat the living shit out of you for that, you . . ."

He smiled, calm as a Sunday morning. "Have you made your decision about the file yet, Jason? It would be good if you did so. I hate indecision. It's irritating."

I leaned close, releasing him, then put my hands on the armrests. "That's what this was about, huh? Helping me make my decision? The brotherhood? Destroying somebody who doesn't deserve to be destroyed? All about me, huh?"

Carter's obsidian eyes bored into me. "Yes, Jason. That is what this is about. Sacrifice. And perhaps you should think about what might happen next if you don't make the right decision."

I stared into those eyes for a moment, my entire body aching to break him in half. I realized then that this wasn't about the Chamber. This was about power. About him. This was about Carter Logan breaking *me* in half, and I didn't know why. "You put him in the Group, leave him alone, write his letter of recommendation, and I'll do it. That's the deal. No other way."

He grinned. "A deal has been made. I will contact him personally, apologize for my insensitive remarks, and let him know he is now a member." With his eyes still on mine and our faces inches apart, a moment passed. "Would you mind taking your face away from me, Jason? I'm uncomfortable with us being this close, and I'd hate to have Kennedy hurt you."

Another moment passed, and I backed off, walking toward the doors. Kennedy smirked, as usual. Carter cleared his throat. "I've anticipated your joining us, Jason, and in the spirit of the Chamber, I've arranged for some help to be given in your task."

"I don't need your help."

He waved me off. "That is all. Dismissed."

CHAPTER SIX

I ARRIVED AT SCHOOL the next morning and caught up to Elvis at the edge of the parking lot. He stood with his huge book bag on his back and two cans of corn in his hands. I waved. "Hey. What's the corn about?"

He looked away, uncomfortable. "You didn't get a call last night?"

"No. About what?"

"There's a food drive today. They called everybody. My mom sent them."

"A food drive?"

"Yeah. I guess some family in town had a tragedy, so Lambert's helping out."

"Huh. They didn't call us." A moment passed. "Did Carter talk to you about the Group?"

He nodded. "He came to my house after the meeting."

"Good. And I'm sorry about what happened. It wasn't you."

"It doesn't matter."

"You're on now, though. And that's what matters for the Pilkney deal, right?"

"Sure."

"And you'll get your letter."

"Don't worry about it."

I looked at him, and my stomach turned uneasy. He'd been crushed yesterday. Carter Logan had ground him to dust, and no matter how much I wanted to act like it didn't happen, it had. "It's not true, you know. Your dad, I mean."

"I'm not ashamed of him. He's a great person."

"I'm sorry. I just . . . You know I don't feel that way, and you know I wasn't behind what happened, right?"

"I don't know what happened, Jason, but I know I don't want to be a part of it."

I sighed. I had everything to do with what happened, I felt like a rotten ass, and now I was paying for it. His face told me he wasn't mad or pissed at me. Worse. Hurt and betrayed. A little bit of fun in the Chamber, all organized by me. Just like with Brooke. Carter was better at this than me, I realized. "I'll make sure he writes the letter, okay?"

He looked at me. "Hey, Jason?"

"Yeah?"

He faltered. "Why'd it happen? Why me? Why does it always have to be me?"

I clenched my teeth. "It wasn't you, Elvis. It was me."

He looked toward the school. "You know what, Jason? It *is* me. I've always been the one, and I know that. I'm the guy, you know? Last picked, never picked, and always the butt of the joke. I was just born that way, and Carter was right. I'm a freak." Then he walked away.

I called after him.

He turned, shaking his head. "I love my father more than the Pilkney Foundation, Jason. I declined Carter. I won't take the letter. Bye." Then he was gone, and I stood there, feeling an inch tall. Elvis had the courage that neither I nor Brooke nor anybody in the Chamber had. He'd looked at a future filled with brilliance, but he'd not been willing to sacrifice what was right. No amount of money could buy the pride he had for his father. A tinge of jealousy ran through me. I wished I had a dad like his.

I walked across the courtyard, up the steps, and into the school. And when I got inside, I saw that the games had begun in full. I stood transfixed, my mind floating in disbelief as I stared.

Every fifth locker down the main corridor had a poster tacked to it, and students milled around, laughing and talking before class began. The Thomas Singletary Food Drive had kicked off today, and as the posters read, canned goods could be donated in the main foyer to help the Singletarys out in their time of need. "To help humanity is to help those who cannot help themselves" was emblazoned across the posters, and below that, my name was listed as the chairman of the committee that organized the drive. I groaned.

Then I walked to the office. Mrs. Pembroke sat behind the counter. I cleared my throat. She looked up, then smiled. "Hello, Mr. Weatherby. How are you today?"

I pointed to the hall. "Who did that?"

51

She furrowed her brow. "Well, Jason, you did. Mr. Kennedy came in this morning with a stack of posters and let me know he was to put them up." She grinned. "Very kind of you to help like that, Jason. When a community cares, it can make all the difference in the world for a family."

I looked at her, realizing she truly had no idea how crappy people could be. "They don't need help. Nothing happened."

"What?"

I squeezed my eyes shut for a moment. "Nothing. Never mind." Then I left, walking down the hall and tearing the posters down. All of them. The bell sounded for first period and I ignored it, scouring the upper floors for anything else, but knowing it was too late. The box in the foyer was half full of beans and corn and soup and any other odd leftover from pantries and cupboards, and Thomas Singletary was the ass end of a big joke at Lambert.

Compliments of me.

CHAPTER SEVEN

"YOU AGREED, DIPSHIT. Take it like a man," Kennedy said. He had a hard time saying it, though, because I had him pinioned against a locker, my hand around his throat. It was more a gravelly squeak.

"I told you I didn't need help. Not this way."

"Did anybody ever let you know you have some serious anger management problems?" he croaked. Some sort of psychotic amusement lit his eyes even as his face turned a shade of red, and I almost pounded him.

"No more, Kennedy. I said I'd handle it, and I will."

"Don't kill the messenger, man. Kill the king." His eyes twinkled. "If you can."

My mind swirled around Elvis and some punk frosh I didn't even like who I was in charge of getting rid of. "He's gone too far, Kennedy. Doesn't that bother you at all?"

Kennedy read my look. "Why do you care, Weatherby?"

"Because this is about Carter hurting people for no reason other than power, and I don't like it."

He craned his neck to the left and right, taking in the gathering crowd of students. "Would you let me go, please? Dissension in the ranks doesn't quite cut the old mustard in the Chamber, and I'm getting tired of not beating the living shit out of you."

I let him go. "I made a deal with Carter, and as far as you're concerned, Kennedy, you're out of it. Out. So stay away from Singletary."

"Or what, Weatherby? Your daddy will raise my taxes?"

"Where is Carter?"

"Not my turn to know."

"Tell him I need to talk."

He scowled. "I'm not your errand boy. Tell him yourself."

I smiled. "That's what you don't get, Kennedy. You are." With that, I left him standing there with his pressed uniform wrinkled and at least forty kids staring at him.

And as I walked toward the double doors, Chancellor Patterson, the ghost of Lambert, wisped toward me. His balding head, what hair was left clinging tightly to his small cranium, glinted under the lights. "Mr. Weatherby. Yes. And how are you? Your father contacted me regarding your acceptance into the Chamber of Five. We had a . . . beneficial conversation."

I stared at his gaunt and pale face. "Who gave the okay for the food drive?"

He smiled. "Why, I did, of course. A grand gesture for this school."

"Who talked to you about it? Carter Logan?"

He frowned. "Perhaps, Mr. Weatherby, a different tone should be taken with me. I am the chancellor, after all." He eyed me. Nobody knew the guy. He was like a wraith around the school, gliding here and there, never talking to students, spending his time cooped up in his office, which we called the cave. I'd been in there only to get busted. "Is there a problem with something?" he said.

"Who talked to you about the food drive?"

He nodded. "The Chamber leadership."

"Kennedy or Carter?"

"Once again, is there a problem?"

"Thomas Singletary doesn't need food, Chancellor Patterson. Nothing happened. No family tragedy. The whole point was to embarrass him, and you gave the okay."

He pursed his lips, still frowning. "I don't know what you're talking about."

I could tell he was sincere, which made him a plain old goofball instead of a malicious freak of nature. "Carter Logan did it to embarrass Thomas because he's poor. It was a joke."

He nodded. "I see. Lambert School for the Gifted is blind to economic status, Mr. Weatherby. I will speak to Mr. Logan concerning your opinion."

"It's not an opinion, and this school isn't blind to anything. Ask the kid if he needs food."

He ignored the jab. "Rest assured I will speak to both. Is that all?"

Woodsie's words about how that file got to the Chamber in the first place came to me, and I knew this was nothing but lip service. I paused, wondering if the chancellor was just a tool or if he really knew what went on.

I decided it didn't matter, though. If they wanted a power play, they could have one, because if I'd learned anything from my dad, it was how to throw other people's weight around. And if Carter was right about one thing, it was that we all had a price.

I looked at the chancellor. "My dad was talking about the new science and technology wing."

He perked up. "Yes, actually, he mentioned it in one of our previous conversations," he said. "We're very excited to get it going."

I nodded. "Yeah. One of his supporters, J. T. Thurmand, you know, from Thurmand Software? Anyway, my dad was throwing around ideas at the table about how to fund it, and J. T. was pretty interested."

"Interested?"

I smiled, low-keying it. "You know how it works with politics, Chancellor. Just talk." I paused. "But you know Thurmand is big-time into school sponsorships."

"Indeed they are."

"Yeah. It sounded like almost a done deal."

"Hmm. Well, perhaps you could ask your father to contact me." He rocked on his heels. "When we spoke before your being chosen for the Chamber, he seemed interested in the new wing. I would do it myself, but I know your father is a busy man."

I smiled. "I'm sure I could talk to him, and by then I'm sure this mess with the food drive will have been taken care of."

His face flattened. "I'm sure it will, Mr. Weatherby, and you can be assured that if any skullduggery has occurred, I will correct the problem."

I walked from the building to the gym after school, gathered my tennis uniform to have it cleaned, then headed to the lot, only to find Carter leaning against the fender of my Mustang. And there, nestled in a cocoon of spider-webbed glass directly in the center of my windshield, lay a big can of Dinty Moore beef stew. Carter shook his head. "Looks like you've got a live one on your hands, Jason."

I sighed. "Did you see him do it?"

"Did I need to see him do it?"

I unlocked the door, throwing my bag in the back. The can fell through the broken glass, bouncing from the stick shift. "Shit."

He laughed. "Kennedy let me know you were . . . upset." His eyes twinkled. "He has marks around his throat."

"They suit him."

He gazed across the parking lot. "You know, Jason, I was thinking that perhaps you've decided to renege on our deal since your friend Elvis declined membership."

I knew I needed time to sort things out. "No, I haven't."

"Good, because a deal is a deal."

"Why Singletary?"

He ignored the question. "You're still on board?"

"Yes."

He cocked an eye at me. "Then why the choke hold on Kennedy? He was . . . flustered about the sudden inability to breathe correctly, and honestly, I'm having a hard time holding him back with you."

"Kennedy is an asshole, and you don't have to hold anything back. If he wants it, I'm here."

He laughed. A genuine, sincere, and throaty thing. "He is quite the anus, isn't he? Sort of like a big, dumb, blabbermouthed penguin. He slobbers when he talks. Disgusting when the saliva gathers at the corners of his mouth, yes?"

"I can't figure you out, Carter."

"What? Me? I'm simple."

"Why are Kennedy and Steven in the Chamber? I can understand Woodside, because he's got a brain and he's a decent guy, but them?"

He studied my face. "Listen, Jason, I know you don't like me. That's a given. And honestly, I don't like you. But you know why we have this problem? It's because we're both strong. Kennedy and Steven aren't. They think they are, but they're not, and that's what makes them useful. They do what they're told if they're made to feel important. Thinking doesn't have much to do with it. And Woodsie, well, Woodsie is the brain behind our budget, and his father, well, that goes without saying, so he's in. It's simple."

"Why me, then? If you knew I'd be a hassle, why?"

A cloud crossed his eyes. "You were chosen because we need strength, Jason. The Chamber is bigger than just me."

"I don't fit."

He shook his head. "Yes, you do."

"Why?"

"Because you are who you are, and though I don't like to admit it, your father has . . . influenced the school quite a bit." He sighed. "Are we done with our little conversation here? I don't like being seen around vandalized property. It makes my skin itch."

"I don't need help with the kid. Stay out of it."

He smirked. "Put up or shut up, Jason, as the saying goes."

"Why does he mean so much to you?"

He stepped away from the car, ignoring me. "I was called into the chancellor's office today about the food drive, Jason. Can I give you some advice?"

I smirked now. "Fire away, Carter."

"You can't hurt me. And if you do anything foolish like that again, you'll pay."

CHAPTER EIGHT

"ARE YOU STILL mad about the windshield?"

Dad didn't turn from the desk in his study, keeping his eyes on the computer screen and tapping a key. "Goddamned computers. I hate them."

"What's the problem?"

"There wouldn't be a problem if I knew what the problem was, would there?"

I walked in, leaning over his shoulder and taking the mouse from his hand. "See? The screen is frozen. Do this." I punched the CTRL, ALT, and DELETE keys, and a box appeared, notifying the user of a nonresponsive program. "You'll lose some material since your last save, but it's the only way I know."

"Just make the damn thing work."

I clicked on the box, and in a minute, the frozen screen disappeared. "Click on the program now."

He did, and it popped up. "Good."

I leaned against the corner of his desk. After the conversation with Carter, I knew he wasn't the one who'd picked me. The orders had come from higher up. "You talked to the chancellor at the beginning of school, didn't you? About the Chamber?"

He nodded, still looking at the screen. You didn't have a conversation with my father. You had a conversation with the back of his head while he was doing something else.

"What about it?" I asked.

"Your new position."

"What did you do, Dad?"

"Son, I've work to do."

"Tell me."

He grunted, then sat back in his chair. "I'm busy, Jason. This session is going to be a war. The Republicans have a good chance at taking control if we don't do some damage control. Can you give it a break for once? Just once?"

"You talked with Chancellor Patterson about the new science and technology wing."

He turned to me. "My son does attend the school, doesn't he? Or rather, I pay a ton of money for him to get mediocre grades while complaining about his spoiled-rotten life."

I sighed. "You made it so I was chosen for the Chamber, didn't you?"

"No."

"What did you do, then?"

He frowned. "I did my job, son."

"Tell me."

He furrowed his brow, irritated. "I pulled strings, Jason, just like you'd do for your son. Like you will do for your son. Is that wrong?"

"What strings?"

"I let the chancellor know that there happened to be a couple of my supporters who had interests in school grants and improvement issues. I offered to direct things his way if things went your way."

I stared at him. My dad's entire life was backroom deals and manipulation, and I had a sudden pang of self-loathing thinking I'd done the very same thing to Patterson today to get Carter in hot water. "And you let him know that the chances of a private donation would be pretty good if I was in the Chamber, didn't you?"

"Son, life is about favors. I take care of the people who take care of me."

"You weren't elected just to care about who takes care of you. That's wrong."

He settled in, and I got ready for another lecture on politics in America. In other words, how to screw people over without making them feel screwed over. For the thousandth time, I made a bet with myself. He'd ask a question next. Every time he was about to go on and on about something, he started with a question. He nodded. "How do you think I win elections?"

I looked at the ceiling. I should be rich. I win bets all the time, I thought. I should move to Vegas and be a professional. "You win elections by knowing the richest people in your district." I shrugged. "They give you money, you use it to plaster yourself all over the place, then you do whatever they want when you win."

He sighed, shaking his head like I was the dumbest idiot in the world. "The *people* vote, Jason. Not just the rich. If the people don't want me doing what I do, it is their right to vote me out. This is America."

"Sure. But they don't know half the crap you do."

"Like what, Jason? Tell me what I do."

"Okay, fine. You're prounion as a Democrat, then you meet with Michael Bosworth two months ago."

He shifted in his seat. "And?"

"And so Bosworth Distributing is moving its headquarters here now."

"So it's wrong bringing business and jobs and money to my district?"

"No. But Bosworth is nonunion."

"I represent *all* of my citizens, Jason. Not just union workers."

"Yeah, sure. So you meet with Bosworth, they get a state-tax break because your enemies, the Republicans, passed a corporate break for new business that *you* voted against, and now Bosworth is competing with your biggest distributing contributor. And nobody can pin a thing on you. Especially the fact that after you met with Bosworth, you invested over a million dollars in the company under Mom's maiden name."

He narrowed his eyes. "My personal business is *mine*. You understand that, Jason? I brought jobs here when we needed jobs. End of story."

"It's wrong."

"It's life. Business. Get used to it."

"You play both sides just to get what you want, and I'm just saying I don't want you to do that at Lambert."

His face darkened. "You have *no* say in what I do or don't do."

I thought about Carter and the Chamber and Chancellor Patterson playing some sort of game, and they all sounded the same. Power. It was all power. I thought about Elvis and his dad, and how they were the ones who were manipulated and used. "I want out of Lambert."

"You belong where I say you do. Now get out. I'm busy," he said, turning away.

CHAPTER NINE

DUE TO A CAN of beef stew decorating my windshield, Mom dropped me off at school, and as I walked across the street, I watched Brooke open her car door. I'd spent the night thinking about what I should do, and she was a part of it. I walked over. "Hi."

She scowled. "Jerk."

I smiled. "I'm still a jerk, huh?"

"You'll always be a jerk."

"I told you I didn't have anything to do with it, and besides, I apologized."

She faced me. "What about that kid? The food drive? I saw the posters. You set it up, and the whole school is laughing at him now. That makes you a jerk."

I couldn't win. "I didn't do it."

She laughed, her voice full of contempt. "Is there anything you don't blame on other people? God, you make me sick."

I winced. "You don't understand, Brooke. I didn't do it."

"Then who did? Somebody set you up? Some sort of conspiracy against the golden child?"

"I'm not a golden child, but yes."

"Why?"

"I don't know."

"Then why are you standing here?"

"Because I like you. And I'm not bad."

Her eyes narrowed, and she clenched her teeth. Then she slapped me. Hard. The sound echoed, and other students stopped, staring as my cheek burned.

Her eyes didn't leave mine as I straightened up. "What was that for?"

"Looking," she said. "And to make it clear that I'll never like you."

I groaned. Talking to this girl was like eating soup with a knife, and simply being around her was painful. But something about her, the way she was, convinced me to stay. "I need your help."

She frowned. "What?"

I studied her. "Why are you at Lambert, Brooke?"

"What does that have to do with anything?"

"Come on. Tell me. Are you gifted? Brilliant? A genius?"

She paused, then her mouth went tight. "So what if I'm not?"

I shrugged. "So I'm not, either."

A long moment passed, and she looked away. "So?"

"So you'll help me if you want to make it so guys like Singletary don't have to put up with this crap."

"So you really didn't do the food drive?"

I nodded. "Meet me after school in the library and I'll tell you more."

CHAPTER TEN

ELVIS LAY SPRAWLED on the gymnasium floor like a dazed pelican, staring at the ceiling. The volleyball-turned-torpedo bounced across the court, and the guy who had spiked it directly into his chest called out, asking if the wounded pelican was okay. Elvis groaned.

I stood over him. "Hey."

"I think I've fractured my sternum," he panted.

I held out my hand. "Here. Get up."

He took my hand as warm-up balls sailed around us. "Thanks."

I looked at him. "We need to talk."

"About what?"

"Meet me in the library after school and I'll tell you."

"I can't."

"Listen, Elvis. I have to make things better. Please?"

He frowned. "I'm not going to be in the Group."

"I know. It's not about that."

"Then what?"

"Just meet me, okay?" I snagged a ball and hit it over the net. "Okay?"

"Sure."

"Good."

After class, I found Mrs. Pembroke sitting behind the office counter, prim and proper, a smile on her face. She reminded me of the ever-happy grandma. World War III could break out and she'd find something to smile about. "Hello again, Mr. Weatherby."

I smiled, letting that famous Weatherby charm that got my dad elected time after time shine through. "Call me Jason, okay? I'm not my dad yet."

She chuckled. "Very well. What can I do for you today, Jason?"

"I'm looking for a copy of the student charter for a project."

She stood, bustling to a file cabinet. "Yes. Of course. Looking up the student policies and rules, I take it?"

"Yes, ma'am."

She came back holding a sheaf of papers stapled together and handed them to me. "There you go, and good luck."

I stuffed them in my bag. "Thanks." I hesitated. "So how is the fund-raising going for the new wing?"

Her eyes brightened. "Very well. It looks like it will be a success."

I nodded. "My dad told me he's working some things up for it. That's cool, huh?"

"It certainly is."

"How much has been raised so far?"

She shrugged. "I haven't looked at the list lately, actually."

I smiled. "Oh yeah. The list. That reminds me. My dad wanted me to get a copy of that for him. He's so excited that people are supporting the cause that he wants to send each and every one an official thank-you letter from his office. He was going to send a staffer over to get it, but since I'm already here, he asked me."

She furrowed her brow. "Hmm. I'm not allowed to hand out financial information like that, Jason. Even if it is for your father."

I took a breath. "Dang. My mom is going to be upset now."

"Your mother?"

I nodded. "She was going to host a cocktail party for the donors. She wants to invite Lambert staff, too." I smiled again. "You know, just to show support for Lambert." I paused, as if thinking. "What if you sealed it in an envelope? My parents were really looking forward to this."

She sighed. "I suppose I could do that. And I know all the donors would love to be recognized for what they've done. Okay." She turned to her computer, clicked into a program, and in a moment leaned over and took a freshly printed list from the machine. She pulled an envelope from a drawer, then folded the list, put it inside the envelope, and sealed it. "There you go."

I slid it next to the charter in my bag. "Thanks, Mrs. Pembroke. I appreciate it."

*   *   *

69

Unlike the study hall, the library was the place to find the dweebs, and it was a discreet location because nobody who was anybody ever went there. Elvis sat at a long table, his book bag open and a quantum physics magazine in his hands. Brooke sat at another table, staring at me as I walked in. I nodded to her, and she stood as I approached. "Thanks for coming."

She smiled. "How's your face?"

"Funny."

"I think so."

I led her to Elvis. "Hey."

He looked up, closing his mag and glancing at Brooke. "Hi."

I sat across the table from him, and Brooke took a seat next to Elvis, introducing herself. A moment passed, and Brooke shrugged. "So why are we here?"

I cleared my throat, looking over my shoulder. "The Chamber needs to be put in its place."

Brooke looked at me. "Soooo . . . you want to be put in your place? You're a member of the Chamber."

I shrugged. "This school isn't what it should be."

"Then why are you in it?" She smirked.

"For the same reason you did what you did. Probably for the same reason half the people in the Youth Leadership Group are in it. Our parents. The pressure. The bullshit."

She flinched, and her jaw muscles worked as she clenched her teeth. Her eyes flicked to Elvis. "That was not fair, Jason. He made me do it—"

Elvis interrupted. "Whoa. Back up. Made you do what?"

Brooke fidgeted.

"Tell him, Brooke," I said.

"No."

"It has everything to do with what is wrong with this place."

She took a moment. "He made me take my shirt off in the Chamber. To get into the Group."

Elvis whistled. "Wow. That's bad."

"I know. And he's making me get that kid, Thomas Singletary, kicked out of Lambert." I looked at Elvis. "That was why Carter brought you in, Elvis. I refused to go after the kid, and he used you to get me to agree."

Brooke stared at me, then stood. "So you really *did* do the food drive thing? God, you're an ass."

"No, no. It's all a power play. I wouldn't do it so they did. It's like a twisted game."

Elvis listened, his big ears like satellites, and Brooke frowned. "So what do you want to do?"

"Will you sit?" I said, looking around.

She did.

I took out the list of contributors to the school, including the donations to the new wing. "This school is screwed up." I put the list on the table. "Look, every new member of the Group this year has a parent connected to that contribution list in a big way, including you, Brooke." I sat back. "Now, look at the general-fund list."

They did, and saw that there were general-fund donations listed from fifty dollars on up to two hundred thousand dollars. Elvis's parents had donated fifty-five dollars. Brooke's mother had donated twenty-five thousand dollars. She saw the comparison and crossed her arms, shifting uncomfortably. Elvis saw his last name and smiled. "My dad worked overtime for that. Pretty cool, huh?"

I nodded, then pulled another list out, one I'd made myself.

"Now, look at this list, and what you'll see is that every single member of the Leadership Group has a parent who has donated at *least* ten thousand dollars . . . compared to the average donation to Lambert of one hundred fifty-six dollars."

Brooke read over the lists, then looked up. "So wealthy people can give more. They should. Your dad gave more than my mom. Way more."

I shook my head. "No. What we're seeing is that you have to buy a place into the Leadership Group in a school meant for *gifted* students, and you know it. We all know it, but we just put up with it. Don't you think that a leadership group at a school for gifted students should be full of . . . gifted students?"

Elvis scratched his head. "What is there to do about it?"

I plopped the school charter on the table. "It's all in there."

Brooke frowned. "Explain."

Elvis nodded. "Yes, please. I'm afraid I don't do well with abstract thought. Please keep it linear."

I looked at him like I knew what that meant, then went on. "When this school began, the regular student council voted who would be a part of the Leadership Group, and it was based on one thing. Academics. But for some reason, they took the academic requirements out when the Chamber of Five was formed. Then it ended up being that the Chamber picked who was in the Leadership Group."

They stared at me.

"So what I'm saying is that in the charter, the regular student council has the power, with a majority vote, to decide who will be in the Youth Leadership Group. *Their* power is higher than the Chamber of Five's, because as far as the charter goes"—I looked at both of them—"the Chamber doesn't exist."

Brooke sat back. "Oh God."

Elvis piped in, "So what? You'll never get the student council to approve a vote on anything. The Chamber rules them."

I shrugged. "Only if those on the student council let them."

Brooke rolled her eyes. "You, Jason, are crazy."

Elvis frowned. "What? What's going on?"

I grinned. "I'm running for president of the student council."

Brooke shook her head. "Besides being insane, you do realize you need a majority approval from the student council? You can't pass anything without three other members' approval." She eyed me. "And if you think even for a split second that I'm going to do anything to jeopardize my position in the Leadership Group, you're nuts. My mom would kill me."

A long moment passed. I took a breath. "I'm asking you both to run with me."

Silence. Dead, black silence. Then Brooke rolled her eyes again. "You must be deaf."

I pleaded. "Come on, guys. It's wrong. They've ruined the school, and it needs to be changed. Carter and his little Chamber need to be put right. Besides Singletary, just think of how many legitimate students have been ripped off over the years because of this crap."

"You can't do it, Jason," Brooke argued. "And even if the three of us made it, you need one more."

Elvis cut in. "Statistically speaking, Jason, my existence is only known to three percent of this school. The odds of me being elected are nil."

Brooke's face turned hard, and I knew what she was thinking, because I'd spent all night thinking about the same thing. Her parents. I leaned forward, staring at her. "Do you belong here, Brooke?"

"Of course I—"

"No, you don't. Just like I don't. Do you know when the last time a *real and qualified-for-this-school* student made it into the Leadership Group? *Decades.* Elvis belongs in it and Thomas Singletary belongs in it, and eighty percent of the students here should be able to strive for it, but they're not allowed. We bought our way in, and you know it. And if eighty percent of the school *knows* that the Chamber will be killed and this school will be what it's supposed to be, they'll vote for us. You know it."

She studied the surface of the table. "I . . . I can't, Jason."

"Don't you think your mother would be proud of you for changing something for the good?"

"Sure, but . . ."

"But what?"

"But if it works, it means . . ."

I nodded. "I know. It means you'd have to give up your spot in the Leadership Group . . . to somebody who deserves it."

Her eyes clouded. "I didn't make Lambert this way."

"But you accept it."

"No, I don't."

"Then prove it."

Elvis piped in, "Academic requirements, huh?"

I nodded.

He smiled. "Well, I don't know about girly-girl here, but I'll

74

join you. And logically thinking, I *could* win a student council spot based on agenda, not on personality."

I stared at Brooke. "You know it's right, Brooke."

She studied the lists on the table, then raised her eyes to Elvis. Moments passed. "Okay. I'm in."

CHAPTER ELEVEN

"I WANT TO KNOW who was in this Chamber." Carter looked around the room, then his eyes fell on me. A bottle of vodka sat in the middle of the table. An empty shot glass with THE BLUE SAPPHIRE scrawled across it was placed upside down over the top of the bottle. "You wouldn't happen to know anything, would you, Jason?"

"I don't know what you're talking about."

Carter studied me intently. "I'm talking about that." He pointed to the bottle.

"A bottle of vodka?"

He nodded. "Yes."

Steven shook his head. "Why would somebody put a bottle of vodka in here?"

Kennedy laughed, rubbing his hands together. "Doesn't matter, Steven. Get the goblets."

Carter stared rivets into Kennedy. "Shut up."

Kennedy shut up.

I frowned. "So what's the big deal? Somebody left a bottle."

"No, Jason. That's not the point. The point is that somebody had the audacity to come in here, and the other point is that they think they can play games with me."

"With a bottle of vodka?"

He stared at me, suspicion in the dark of his eyes. Silence filled the room.

"I didn't do it. Why would I do it?"

He didn't answer, but spoke to all of us. "I want whoever did this in front of me by tomorrow. Got it?"

Kennedy sighed. "Dude, aren't you being a little bit paranoid? It's a bottle, Carter. And it may just be a gift, even if they did come in here unauthorized. Let's drink it."

Carter shook his head, contempt oozing from his mouth. "Kennedy, if I want advice from a pile of shit, I'll consult a horse's ass. Be quiet. And if you ever call me *dude* again, I'll have you neutered."

Frowning, Kennedy sat back. "I didn't mean—"

Carter slammed his palm on the table, his eyes blazing, his neck strained. "SHUT THE FUCK UP! I want whoever did this in front of me by tomorrow after school! Got it?"

Kennedy stepped back, putting his hands into his pockets. "Yeah, Carter. Sure. I got it."

I caught up to Woodsie on the front steps after we'd adjourned, completely confused about what had just happened. "Hey."

He turned. "Hey."

"What was that all about?"

Woodsie smiled. "Somebody is having fun. Dangerous fun."

"With a bottle of vodka? How?"

Woodsie looked back at the school. "Remember I told you Carter's father was thrown off the bench?"

"Yeah. For drunk driving."

He nodded. "Yeah. He'd been drinking vodka tonics all night."

"So what? Is Carter that neurotic to think that's what the bottle meant?"

Woodsie's eyes met mine. "He's not being neurotic."

"Why?"

Woodsie stared across the grounds. "Because the name of the bar he was drinking at before they nailed him was The Blue Sapphire."

I whistled, remembering the shot glass. "Whoa."

"Yeah, whoa. That's the closest I've ever seen him to going ballistic, Jason. He's on the edge."

"I didn't do it."

"He thinks you did."

"I didn't even know."

He shrugged. "What you know doesn't really matter, Jason. What I know, on the other hand, is that you and Carter have issues. Big ones."

I stared off across the street, watching traffic pass. "The only reason I'm in the Chamber is because of my dad getting this school money for the new wing."

"I wasn't born yesterday. I know why I'm in the Chamber, too."

"And you're okay with that?"

He sighed, facing me. "Jason, what you're not understanding is that what I'm okay with and what you're okay with doesn't matter. We have absolutely no way of controlling what happens here. Our parents do, and they control it through the list."

"You know about the donation list?"

"Yes. The Chamber president picks new members from it each year. It's tradition."

"So that's why Carter doesn't like me?"

He nodded. "See, Carter *has* to pick the highest on the list, so he had to pick you. And you represent a threat." He looked away. "You're different."

I thought about it for a minute. "If you could change the Chamber, would you?"

He didn't answer.

"Would you?"

"I don't know."

I almost spilled my guts out to him, but I decided I wasn't ready. Not yet. I had something to take care of first.

"Why, Jason?"

I blew it off. "No reason. Just sucks what we have to do sometimes, you know?"

"Sure does."

CHAPTER TWELVE

I SAT ACROSS THE CAFETERIA table from Thomas and watched him eat a bologna sandwich. I'd been sitting there for minutes, and we'd not said a word to each other. Bite, chew, swallow. Nothing else. We were playing a game. His eyes never left mine. I cleared my throat, finally tired of the game. "I might have come on a bit strong the other day."

He set his sandwich down, meticulously dabbing crumbs from the table with his finger and flicking them at me. I ignored it. He burped. "Get a new windshield yet?"

I shrugged. "I know you did it, and I don't blame you. But I didn't have anything to do with the food drive."

He smiled. "If somebody screwed with my car, they'd pay. Big-time pay."

"You're not me."

"Thank God. I'd hate to be a coward," he said, opening up a baggy of Fritos.

I sighed. "You hate this school, right?"

"No. I love it. And I love you. In fact, I think I'm gay for you. Want to make out?"

"I'm serious, Thomas."

"Me too. I want your tongue in my mouth."

I cleared my throat. "I want you to run for student council with me."

He chuckled. "Why would I do that?"

I looked around, lowering my voice, knowing I was taking a big chance. If word got out too soon, I'd be smoked. "Because I'm running for student council president and I need a majority vote if we win."

"Majority vote on what?"

"To get rid of the Chamber and make it so that regular students are in control of the Youth Leadership Group." I paused. "And so crap like the food drive doesn't happen anymore."

He hesitated, his hand stopping for just a moment as he grabbed a chip. "You're part of the Chamber."

"I know."

"And you want to get rid of it."

"Yes."

He chuckled again. "Didn't take you for emo. You like hurting yourself?"

"It's wrong."

"So you choose a guy who hates you."

I smiled. "You hate me because of what I am."

"True."

"I'm trying to get rid of what I am at this school."

"You aren't as stupid as I thought."

"We don't have to be friends to achieve a common goal, Thomas."

"You sound like a politician already."

"Comes with the territory. Are you in?"

"So you have a master plan, huh?"

"Yes. And it'll work."

"Tell me one thing," he said.

"What?"

"Most people don't enjoy kicking themselves in the face. You really want to hurt yourself?"

I cocked an eye at him. "You really want my tongue in your mouth?"

"No."

I nodded. "Then we're mutually agreed."

"So you want me to help you kick yourself in the face."

"Yes."

"Then I'm in."

CHAPTER THIRTEEN

"I'M DROPPING THE CHAMBER." I almost barfed when I said it, and two hours of sitting in my room trying to find the guts to do it hadn't made anything easier. It would start raining bombs now.

He didn't turn. "No you're not."

I took a breath, careful with my words. "I don't fit in with it, Dad. It's not me."

He did turn then, and clasped his hands across his belly. He clenched his jaw, and those sheet-metal eyes, hard and impenetrable, blocked everything. "It's not you? What does that have to do with what I say?"

I looked away. I could never look him in the eye when I knew he was really going to get pissed, and I hated myself for it. "Dad, it's just—"

"It's JUST NOTHING!" he bellowed, his neck flushing instantly, like a thermometer stuck in a pit of magma. He stood, jabbing a finger at me. "You sit in this house surrounded by everything a teenager could ever want, and you have the nerve to pull this?" He pointed out the window. "There are people out there with *nothing*, and you just don't get that, do you? You don't get that the world isn't a nice place, Jason, because you've never lived on that side of things, have you?" His eyes seared my soul, and his voice boomed through the house. "HAVE YOU?"

I sighed. "No."

"Then shut your mouth."

I looked away. "I just—"

He cut me off. "Why do you think I do this? Why do you think I'm down your throat all the time? You think I like it?"

"No."

"Then why? Tell me, Jason. I know what you see when you look at me, son, so why don't you tell me why I put myself through this."

"I don't know."

He sneered. "Well, I know. It's because you don't have courage. I have a coward for a son."

"I'm not a coward."

He came close, towering over me. "Then look me in the eye and tell me what you think of me."

I couldn't do either. "I just want to go to a regular school."

He took a deep breath and cleared his throat. "You're staying in the Chamber."

Carter flashed through my mind, and Thomas Singletary tailed along behind him. I felt sick, but I couldn't look him in the eye. His breath hit my cheek. I swallowed. "No, I'm not."

The slap, harsh and sharp and hard, echoed through the

silent room. My eye watered, I saw stars and blackness, and my cheek burned with a numb and deep throb. I tasted blood, wondering as I stared at the floor if his hand hurt. Brooke had nothing on him.

His presence was like a huge and dark cloud over me. "You will remain in the Chamber. You will maintain your grades. You will do exactly as I tell you to do, Jason, or God help me, I'll put you on the street."

CHAPTER FOURTEEN

I GOT UP EARLY the next morning, padded downstairs, and lifted my keys from the kitchen counter.

"Jason?"

I turned, and Mom stood in the entry, clutching a robe around her. "Hi."

She looked at my face, at the busted lip, and glanced away, just like every other time it had happened. If I got a sliver she'd be all over it; making sure I was okay, getting the tweezers and finding the alcohol to make sure it didn't get infected. She was the queen mother bee hovering over me, and always had been. Unless my dad hit me. Then she ignored it. Just like she ignored it when he hit her.

When I was little, I didn't understand. I thought she didn't care. I wondered why she didn't tell him to stop. To never do it again. But now I knew. She was just like me. Afraid. But it still pissed me off. She fake-yawned. "It's early. Do you have a makeup test or something?"

"Yeah," I lied.

She strode forward. "Here, let me get you something to eat," she said, taking a box of cereal down from the top of the refrigerator.

I shook my head. "I'm fine."

"You should really have a good breakfast before—"

"Why the fuck do you care about what I eat?" I touched my lip. "See this, Mom? See it? I can't eat because Dad busted it open, and you know what? I don't want a fucking thing from you or anybody else anymore." Then I grabbed my bag and left her standing there, the horrified and hurt look on her face haunting me as I walked out.

CHAPTER FIFTEEN

"CAMPAIGNING BEGINS TOMORROW, election in a week," Elvis said as we walked. "That's forty-two school hours to win, but the equivalent of three brains working on it triples the efficiency factors."

"Uh, sure. Cool," I said, still preoccupied with why I'd spoken to my mom the way I had. We passed a section of the hall where a candidate was taping up a poster. VOTE KILKENNY FOR TREASURER. MAKE YOUR MONEY WORK FOR YOU.

"Are you sure about this, Jason?"

I nodded. "Yeah. We can do it. Have you been making your posters?"

"I have. I'm scared to put them up, though. People will draw on them or something."

"We'll do it tomorrow. Together," I said. Brooke and I were meeting after school to make our signs, and I was looking forward to it. "Did you register?"

"Yes. So did Brooke."

"Cool."

He hesitated. "Uh, you saw her boobs?"

I remembered what I'd said in the library. "It wasn't a good thing, Elvis."

He nodded quickly. "Well, yeah, of course not. But you saw them?"

I sighed. "Yes."

"Wow. Were they . . ." He stopped when I glared at him, then thought better of it. "Wow."

"She's pretty."

"You like her?" He smiled.

"Yeah, I do. Not just because of that, but yeah."

"Yeah."

I chuckled. "Never seen live boobs before, huh?"

"Nope. Just in the movies and stuff."

I hadn't, either, and a knife of guilt sliced through me as I thought about her. I was supposed to be sickened by it, and I was, but not *all* of me was. "It wasn't a good way to see 'em for the first time."

He screwed his eyes up. "You're kidding, right? I'm a math genius with the social skills of a toad, Jason. Unless I go to some strip joint, I'll never see any."

I laughed. "I'm sure there's a few math-genius babes out there," I said, then noticed a group of people gathered in the hall. We walked up to them, and I stood, staring at the wall, stunned.

There, taped to the wall, was a two- by three-foot poster board. Half of it was plastered with a blown-up photograph of Judge Logan, father of Carter Logan. He was behind his bench, regal and stern in his black robe, gavel in hand, sentencing a criminal. Below it, the caption read: JUDGE LOGAN SENTENCING A DRUNK DRIVER.

Beside that, covering the other half of the poster board, was the mug shot of a very drunk and disheveled Judge Logan. It looked like his crumpled collar was stained with vomit, and drool glistened on his chin. Below, the caption read: FORMER JUDGE LOGAN, DRUNK SCUM.

Elvis shook his head. "Is that Carter's dad?"

I nodded, shocked to silence. My stomach squirmed.

"Holy shit!" A voice came from behind us.

I turned, and Kennedy stood there, smiling as he stared at it. He looked at me. "You must have a death wish. I hate your guts, but, man, you're my hero. Your balls must be so big—"

"I didn't do it," I interrupted.

He chuckled, studying the poster with his finger under his chin. "What'cha think? The left or the right look better? I personally like the mug shot. The grainy quality and the stupor seem to dig deep into personality. Puke is always good, too. Adds depth. There's a human quality to it."

I sighed. Trouble. This was big-time trouble.

Elvis shuffled. "Maybe you should take it down, Kennedy."

He crossed his eyes, mocking Elvis. "Why? This is art, my geeky and freaky spaghetti noodle of a person friend. Weatherby's got quite an eye for it."

From behind, another voice. This one a sinister slither. "Do as he says, Kennedy."

We turned, and Carter stood there, his face flushed, his hands clenched into fists. Kennedy took it down, not a little fear in his eyes. "Dude, I was just about to take it down. Malicious stuff."

Carter looked at me, his eyes black as night. He said nothing, just stared. "The Chamber at four today," he said, finally, then turned, walking away.

I had planned, gladly and with extremely nervous pleasure, to drop two bombs in the Chamber today. One was to quit, which I wouldn't do because I couldn't deal with my dad right now, and the other was to announce my candidacy for student council president. Neither would happen, though. Not yet. I had an inkling of an idea, and if it worked, I could do this. I could make it work.

Today, I knew, I'd have a hot iron put to me. I saw that look in Carter's eyes, and there was no question who he thought was after him. Me.

When I entered the Chamber, everybody but Carter was present. Woodsie sat silent, his chiseled jaw set impassively; Steven slouched, his ferret eyes darting around; and Kennedy, of course, split his face open with a toothy grin when he saw me. "'Sup, Weatherhead. I was just thinking of what your obituary would read."

I shook my head. "Save it, Kennedy."

He laughed. "For what? The only thing I'm saving is to give to your mother. Man, I'd like to—"

I lunged forward, grabbing his collar with both fists and ramming him back in his seat. His head snapped against the cushion of the leather chair, and he grunted in shock. Silence filled the room. "I'm going to break your face if you say one more word about her, Kennedy. Got it?"

He smiled. "Dude, you did not just assault me, did you? You did not just do something that you will regret in a big way, right?" He swiveled his head to Steven Lotus. "Have I just been assaulted?"

I stared into his eyes, still clutching his shirt.

He sighed, a crestfallen look coming to his face. "Okay. Fine. I crossed a line about your mom and I'm sorry." Then he grinned. "But can I talk about your new girlfriend and her booby show? It's like a movie caught on replay in my mind, and I don't even have to throw a dollar on the stage."

Rage coursed through me like a flash flood in a thunderstorm: lightning-strike images of my father hitting me, my mother cowering like a scared kitten, Carter and his goddamn eyes staring into mine as Elvis skulked from the Chamber. My stomach clenched in shame even as my veins pumped with hate. I let go of Kennedy's shirt and stepped back. "Stand up."

Kennedy blinked, licking his lip.

I nodded. "Stand up, Kennedy. Now."

He smiled. "This isn't the place for—"

I swung, smacking his face so hard the firecracker slap of it echoed against the walls. His eyes glazed over for a moment, blood running down his chin. Seconds passed. He did nothing, just sat there, blinking. He touched his lip, then tasted his blood.

In another second, he lunged from the chair, barreling into me like a linebacker crushing a practice pad. We crashed to the floor in a tangle of arms and legs, his weight pinioning me to the carpet as he pounded my ribs. I twisted, grabbing the sides of his head and slamming his face to the floor as I slithered from underneath him. As he rose, I swung, landing a solid shot against his ear. Then Woodsie was on me, yanking me away.

"Enough," he said, standing between us. My ribs ached even

as Kennedy's broken lip sent a shiver of ugly pleasure up my spine.

Kennedy stood as I got up. He clenched his teeth, his chest heaving. "You've had it, Weatherby."

"Keep your mouth shut and we're fine, bitch."

"We're not fine."

"Looks like I missed something," a voice said.

We turned, and Carter stood at the door. He leaned against the hinges. "Kennedy, you're dribbling blood on your uniform."

Kennedy wiped his mouth.

Carter entered. "I'd say a mediation session was in order, but being that I wouldn't mind watching you kill each other, let's at least keep the bloodshed outside. These carpets are expensive."

Kennedy grunted. "Asswipe bitch-slapped me."

Carter took a seat at the table. "Stop being a bitch, then." A moment passed. Silence. He spoke as we joined him at the table. "The business at hand is this: The student council campaign has begun, and as I had planned, most of the candidates will be compliant to our wishes. I've interviewed them, and some are already in the Youth Leadership Group, which plays to our favor. There are five who are not compliant, but they shouldn't be a problem. I've got people on it." He paused. "I've also arranged for William Hennessy, a member of the Leadership Group, to run for president in opposition to Steven here. He's quite popular, and has agreed to pull out of the race at the last moment. . . ." Carter smiled. "Call it an insurance policy on Steven's success." He went on. "Jules Tupper, the other presidential candidate, is not a part of anything and won't be a problem. If he is, Kennedy will take care of the problem."

Kennedy smiled, staring at me. "My pleasure."

Carter went on. "Now we'll move into something personal, which I'm sure you are all aware of. Somebody is out to harm the Chamber, and we've got to stop it."

Steven shook his head. "Somebody is after you, Carter. Not the Chamber."

Carter breathed, his face soft and gentle. "No, Steven, you don't understand. The brotherhood relies on each member to create the strength of the entire Chamber. Yes, this individual may be targeting me, but it's obviously a plan wrought from the mind of a jealous person. A student who opposes the Chamber and what we stand for. I've no doubt we will all be targeted if we allow it to continue." He looked at me. "We can't allow it to continue. Can we, Jason?"

I seethed. "Say it if you're going to say it, Carter."

"Say what?"

"That you think I'm doing it."

He nodded. "I do, as a matter of fact. I see the motivation, I see you challenging the laws of the Chamber, and I see your obvious dislike of me."

"I'm not doing it."

"Prove it," he said.

"I can't."

"Yes, you can. You can prove your loyalty once and for all to the Chamber."

"How? By getting Thomas Singletary out of Lambert?"

Carter sighed. "Things have gone beyond that. I think we're at a pivotal moment where your integrity needs to be fully established." He eyed me. "And I think you need to realize just how serious this is."

I tensed.

Carter stood, easing his chair back and walking to a hutch. He opened a drawer and brought out something cylindrical, then came to the table and sat. He laid it on the wood surface. It was a lead pipe, about a foot and a half long. "This is filled with cement. Tomorrow at lunchtime, Thomas Singletary will be brought to the south-wing restroom, where you will be waiting for him. Kennedy here will place Mr. Singletary's arm across the seat of a toilet, and you will break his arm with the pipe. You will then direct him to find another school immediately."

My insides deflated like a gut-shot buck. "No."

He leveled a stare at me. "You brought this on yourself. You could have taken care of things without violence, but you chose not to choose. Now I choose for you."

Woodsie fidgeted, but said nothing.

I shook my head. "No. The deal's off."

"It will happen with or without you, Jason."

"Fuck you."

"You will be removed from the Chamber. And disgraced."

I raised my head, staring at Carter. "Once you're a member of the Chamber, you cannot be removed unless you leave the school voluntarily or are expelled. It's in your own *unofficial* charter that your own stinking grandfather made up, so eat me, Carter. I'm not going anywhere."

His face turned a shade of red. "Why are you doing this?"

"I'm not touching Thomas Singletary, and if you do, I'll report it."

"You have no power here, Jason."

I laughed, my rage suddenly . . . liberating. I was beyond caring. "You think your drunk dad has power over me? You think

95

you do?" I stood, leaning over the table. "Come on, Carter, you know how the game works, right? Well, here's the deal. You touch Singletary and I *will* be after you."

Carter took a moment, then began clapping. Slowly. He looked around the table. "Anybody else care to join the mutiny? Speak now."

Silence. Uncomfortable, nervous silence. Even Kennedy's face went blank, the sarcastic smirk gone.

Carter spoke. "Are you done whining, yet, Jason? You have your orders, and you will follow them."

I stared at him, knowing the terms of battle were clear. Then I walked out.

CHAPTER SIXTEEN

BROOKE SMILED WHEN I met her at my car after school. "New windshield?"

"You heard?"

"Who didn't hear?"

"Typical."

"I also heard that you were the one who put up the judge poster." She eyed me. "Did you?"

"Does it matter?"

"To me it does."

"No, I didn't."

"You two have some issues, don't you?"

I shrugged. "We don't get along."

"Be careful around him, Jason."

I told her about the plan to break Singletary's arm, and she looked down, silent.

"Mind if we make a stop before doing the posters?" I said.

She nodded. "I'm free until dinner."

We drove, talking about the election, the platform that we'd campaign on, and school in general. She was nervous to be taking on the Chamber, and hadn't dared to tell her mother yet. I reached to the backseat at a stoplight, grabbing Thomas Singletary's file and handing it to her. "His address is inside."

"Warning him?"

I nodded.

She looked at me, hesitating. "Did I do that much damage to your lip?"

I rubbed my tongue over the slightly swollen cut. "I ran into a door."

She frowned. "Lame."

"What?"

"You're a horrible liar."

I shrugged. "My dad."

Silence.

"You don't want lies, but you don't want the truth, either. Not fair."

"He hit you?"

"Yeah."

"I'm sorry."

I shrugged, brushing it off. "He lost his temper."

"You told him about the Chamber?"

I nodded.

She looked out the window. "Maybe I didn't want to know the truth."

"He's not that bad. Just when he's around."

She didn't laugh. "He's a congressman."

I laughed at that one. "And that's supposed to make him any different?"

"Does he do it often? Hit you?"

"No. It's been around a year since the last time."

That seemed to make her feel better. On-and-off hitters were better than all-the-time hitters, I guess, and as we drove, I glanced at her profile. She was pretty. She noticed me looking. "What?"

I drove. "Nothing."

"You were looking at me."

"I'm not some kind of abused kid, Brooke. We just got into it. That's all."

"Okay."

I shifted. "He's just an asshole. The world is full of them."

"He shouldn't hit you."

I cleared my throat. "So are you going to give me the address or are we going to drive around all day talking about the social ramifications of dickhead dads?"

She finally laughed, shaking her head, then gave me the address.

Slum city. I'd been through the Heights before, but it was different when you pulled from the main arterials and drove through the neighborhoods. Blocks of small houses, most with hash-brown front yards, led to concrete apartment buildings and complexes looking like cold-war-era bomb shelters. Guys hung on corners talking trash and giving hard stares as we passed, and I began having second thoughts.

This was what my dad called a necessary evil. On a grand

scale, these were the losers of society, and to have winners you needed losers. He'd told me once that keeping the losers centralized in areas like the Heights protected the regular people and gave the cops something to do other than handing out speeding tickets and sleeping in their cruisers.

We found Thomas's apartment building, a thirteen-story concrete box on D Street, and I glanced around, unsure I wanted to be there. My brand-new red Mustang GT stuck out like the last ripe cherry on the tree, and I figured we had around ten minutes before it'd get 'jacked. Brooke looked around, then spoke. "Are you sure . . ."

"No. Not really." I took a breath, pulling to the curb.

"We should leave, Jason."

"I need to warn him."

Just then, a guy in ass-dragging Lakers shorts and a white tank top bent down to my window. "What you need?"

I shook my head. "No thanks, man."

He kept walking, his eyes lingering on the car. Brooke rolled her window up, and I looked at her. "Maybe I should take you home first."

"No."

"You sure?"

"We're already here, and I refuse to be judgmental."

I rolled my eyes. "Too late, you elitist."

"You're no better."

I nodded, opening the door. "Come on. We'll just go up, knock, tell him what's up, then split."

"Can't you just call him?"

"I tried. Disconnected."

She looked around. "What about your car?"

"Want to stay in it?"

She looked around. "No."

I smiled. "They can have it for all I care. Come on. We'll walk fast." I got out, and after a moment, Brooke hopped out, shut the door, and came around. We walked down the sidewalk, past an old Chevy Corsica with one wheel missing and a concrete block holding the axle up, and entered the building. "At least he's on the first floor. Twenty-three."

She nodded, quickening her step down the hall, and soon we stood in front of his door. I knocked.

No answer. I knocked again, and a moment later, a little girl, probably around ten years old, answered, opening the door a crack and peeking out. She didn't say anything, just stared with that one big brown eye.

"Hi. Is Thomas here?" Brooke smiled.

The eye narrowed. "No."

Brooke leaned down to her eye level, smiling like some concerned social worker or teacher. "Will he be back?"

"Duh. He lives here."

"Oh, dumb me. When will he be back?"

"Do I look like his babysitter?"

I choked down a laugh. Brooke went on. "No, you look like a pretty little girl. Do you know where he is?"

With that, her eye slid over and her tongue, stuck out at us, showed pink and spitty. "No." Then the door slammed shut.

Brooke flinched, straightening. I laughed. "You're good with kids."

"Spare me."

"No, you are. You really connected with her. I loved the way she slammed the door in your face."

She sighed. "Then you try, jerk."

I shook my head. "She'd shoot me. Let's go," I said, and as we walked out and down the sidewalk toward the car, I saw something.

Michael Woodside, dressed down in Levis, Nikes, and a T-shirt, ducked into an alley at the end of the building.

CHAPTER SEVENTEEN

THE NEXT MORNING, arriving at school, I answered my cell and Woodsie's voice came through. "You here?"

I grabbed my pack from the passenger seat and watched as students filed into the building. My political posters lay on the backseat, and I'd arrived early to tack them up. Brooke and Elvis were supposed to be doing the same. "Yeah. Why?"

"Come to the Chamber." Then he hung up.

I left the posters and walked, nervous, my mind on seeing Woodsie last night in the Heights, uncomfortable with what was going on in the Chamber, and worried sick about Carter following through on his threat against Thomas. I had to find him before they did. My pace quickened, and by the time I got there, my pulse was actually racing.

I stood outside the doors to the Chamber, trying to ease the flood of anxiety coursing through me. Was it a trap? I wondered.

I put my hand on the knob, turning it, and as I stepped inside, silence. Woodsie sat in his chair at the table, alone, staring at the object sitting there. His eyes met mine, then went back to the centerpiece.

The lead pipe from the day before stood on end. A single red rose, the stem taped around the top of the pipe, bloomed. I furrowed my brow. "What's up with that?"

"I was hoping you could tell me, Jason."

I looked at the lead vase with the flower on it and shook my head. "I have no idea."

"This is bad, Jason."

"What? That somebody dared come in here again?"

"You didn't hear what happened, did you?"

"No."

He stared at me. "Somebody left a note for Carter last night about who was playing games with him. They wanted a meeting. Said they'd tell him for a hundred dollars."

"And?"

He gestured to the rose. "They wanted to meet in the rose garden at Manito Park."

"What happened?"

"Carter showed up, and whoever it was broke his arm." He pointed to the pipe. "With that."

"Did he see who?" I said, hoping against hope that he had.

"No. It was dark, and the guy was wearing a ski mask. Carter called me last night when he got home from the hospital. The guy came from behind, nailed him in the back, pinned him down, then slammed his arm three times."

I groaned.

"Then I get here this morning, and this is sitting here like a present. I saw Carter put it away after you left, man, and now we have a problem. A big one."

I stared.

He stood. "It's one of us, Jason. It has to be. Who else would know about the pipe? Who would know Carter told you to break that kid's arm today? It's a member of the Chamber, Jason." He studied me.

"It's not me."

He looked away, uncomfortable. "Then who? You're the only one who has a beef with him."

I paused. "I saw you yesterday in the Heights."

He didn't say anything.

I set my jaw. "What were you doing there?"

Silence.

"Don't bullshit me, Woodsie. Carter sent you there for some reason, didn't he?"

He shook his head. "If you're the one, Jason, I'm not having anything to do with it. I can't help you."

I raised my eyebrows. "If I'm the one? You were in the Heights last night. What were you doing there? And what were you doing here this morning?"

He sat back down. "Just answer my question, Jason. Are you doing this?"

"Answer mine. Where do you stand with all of this?"

He looked at me. "I could ask the same damn thing. Why were you in the Heights?"

I grunted. "We're done talking."

A moment passed before he spoke again. "I was going to warn the kid about today, but he wasn't home."

"Well, so was I. And you've obviously got a problem with the situation, too, so why couldn't it be you who is gunning for Carter?"

"I'm where I'm at today because I know when to keep to myself, which you don't know how to do."

"Then why try to warn him?"

"Because there's a difference between—"

"Taking a picture of a blow job and a broken arm?" I said. "You're kidding me, Woods. Right?"

He looked away. "Don't pin that on me, man. I took the picture. That's all. And besides, I wouldn't do it now. I was scared. And dumb. I was new to the Chamber and everything was crazy."

I shrugged. "There's no way I can be sure you didn't break his arm, Woods, and you can't be sure I didn't do it. So where does that leave us?"

He shook his head. "Not my style and you know it. I'm out of here at the end of the year, Jason. I've no reason to have a beef with anybody. Singletary or Carter."

"But it's *my* style?"

He smiled. "Dude, you jacked Kennedy in the face. I've never even hit another person."

I sighed. "This has to be stopped."

"Make a deal?" he said.

"What deal?"

"Like I said, I'm out of this school at the end of this year and I've got nothing to lose by just keeping my mouth shut about everything. Then I'm free and clear. College, no more dad, and I can live the way I want to. Same goes for you after another year, huh?"

"What's your deal?"

"That we trust each other, and that we work together to find out who is doing this. On the sly. Then we deal with it."

"You're afraid he thinks you're in on it, huh?"

"I think anything could happen, but I know Carter would nail a dozen people just to get one, and I have no plans of being on the list. I'm protecting me. Remember that."

"This is wrong, Woodsie."

"I know it is. And that's part of why I called you."

"No, I mean the Chamber. This school. The Youth Leadership Group. It's all wrong."

"What are you saying?"

"I'm saying that as of this morning, I'm running for student council president, and I'm going to change it all."

He gaped at me. "What?"

"Yeah. I'm doing it. The Chamber has no official power at this school, and I'm going after it."

"Why not just kill yourself now?"

I shrugged. "I'm sure my dad will for me, but it's wrong. The real students have no power."

He nodded. "Not that it matters, because it won't work, but what's your platform?"

"Academic requirements will dictate who is a member of the Youth Leadership Group, and the Chamber will be reorganized as the board overseeing the YLG. Leadership Group open voting will decide who sits in the Chamber."

"You're crazy."

I smiled. "The school charter doesn't even recognize the Chamber." I looked at him. "I'd appreciate it if you'd keep it to yourself for now."

"Sure. But you know I can't help you. I can't risk my dad cutting me off."

I smiled again. "Wimp."

He smirked. "That sounds weak, huh?"

"It sounds like life," I said, then chuckled. "But it is weak."

"I'll give you a heads-up on anything I hear, huh?"

"Sure."

CHAPTER EIGHTEEN

I TACKED UP the last of my posters, this one in the cafeteria, and the buzz was already beginning. Between the three of us, we'd plastered the school. All the posters read the same. One thing. A promise to change the school charter to base admittance to the Youth Leadership Group and the Chamber of Five on academics and school involvement. Open voting by the Youth Leadership Group to choose the members of the Chamber of Five. Lambert was a school for the brilliant, and the leadership of the school should be representative of that. Our slogan was PUT THE POWER IN YOUR HANDS!

I should have been happy, but I was just plain miserable. I'd committed myself to something huge, and honestly, I was scared. This wasn't the way I did things. Jason Weatherby stood in the background, unconcerned and to himself. Now I was front and center, and my stomach complained about it. That, and Thomas Singletary was nowhere to be found.

As I turned to leave the cafeteria, Carter faced me. I don't know how long he'd been standing there. His right arm was casted and in a sling, and his face was as hard as the lead pipe that had busted the bone. "So this is it, huh?" he said, motioning to the poster.

I nodded.

"You're going to pay, Jason."

"I'm changing this school. You can't touch me."

He smiled a wicked smile. "I'm not going to touch you, Jason"—he raised his cast—"just like you didn't touch me."

I frowned. "I don't care if you think I did it or put somebody up to it or whatever. I didn't. You're a psycho."

"And I don't care if you didn't do it, Jason. As I said before, we're beyond that. You've started something you can't stop."

"Go to hell."

He smiled again. "You have no idea where I am, Jason. None." Then he turned, walking away.

CHAPTER NINETEEN

BROOKE AND I sat under an elm tree in the courtyard during lunch. She brought out a croissant stuffed with cream cheese, ham, and sprouts. "Who broke his arm, Jason?"

"I don't know."

"Well, it's got to be somebody."

I took a swig of Gatorade. "You don't trust me, do you?"

She ate.

"Tell me."

She swallowed, taking a moment. "The truth?"

"Yes."

"You and Carter hate each other, for one. For two, I could see anybody breaking his arm as some sort of justice for ordering Singletary's arm broken, and for three, you come from a home with violence in it." She glanced away. "I also heard about the fight you and Kennedy got into."

I screwed the cap on my Gatorade and stood. "For one, Brooke, I don't need your analysis of my life. For two, unlike you, my family isn't all daisies and tulips, and for three, you don't know shit about anything in my house."

She blinked. "I'm sorry. I didn't mean to . . ."

"To what? Judge me? Sort of like I *didn't* judge you in the Chamber? Or *are* you a slut?"

Her chin quivered. "I didn't mean it that way."

"Well, it came out that way, and I don't need it. I don't lie, Brooke. I might be a coward and a slacker and everything else my dad says, but I'm not a liar."

She took a deep breath, picking a sliver of grass and rolling it between her fingers. "You're right. I trust you. I just don't know what's going to happen."

I sat. "Me neither."

"What if he goes after me? Or Elvis?"

"Then I'll kill him," I said, instantly regretting it. "Figuratively, I mean."

"My mom is going to kill me when she finds out what we're doing."

"Figuratively?"

She laughed. "Yes."

"Are you still on board?"

She nodded. "Elvis is uncontrollably nervous, Jason. When we were putting up our posters this morning, he excused himself to the bathroom to be sick."

I chuckled. "He'll do fine."

"We still need a majority to do this, you know. If we only carry three seats, it's not enough to bring a vote."

I looked across the courtyard, where students gathered and wandered and hustled here and there. "Thomas Singletary."

"What?"

"He's running for a council position."

Her eyes widened. "Joke of the year, right? He hates you."

I nodded. "He might hate me, but he hates this school more."

"Nobody knows him. He's a mystery around here." She paused. "A freaky one."

"People aren't going to vote for *somebody*, Brooke, they're going to vote for a cause. Just like with Elvis."

"What about the Chamber? They must know by now."

"The Chamber can screw off."

A moment passed before she spoke. "Does Carter still think it's you?"

"I don't think it matters to him now. He's off his rocker, and I think even if he knew it wasn't me, he'd still be gunning for me."

She grunted. "You said the only people who knew about the pipe were in the Chamber."

"Yep."

She glanced at me. "Woodsie?"

"I don't know, Brooke. He said no, but it's not like anybody is going to admit it. For all I know, Kennedy and Steven hate his guts, too."

Just then, Chancellor Patterson floated across the courtyard, saw us, and came over. He smiled. "Jason, Brooke, wonderful to see both of you."

We stood, shaking his hand. "Sure."

"Your father called me this morning about the new wing,

Jason, and I congratulated him on your running for president of the student council." He paused, then went on. "He seemed . . . unaware of it. And of the innovative platform you, and your friends, of course, are running on."

I groaned. Dead. My dad was going to kill me. Taking a breath, I erased the images flashing in my head of all the different and creative ways he could make me not living. Then it occurred to me what it felt like to know you've got nothing to lose. I met his eyes. "It is innovative, huh? We were just talking about how much the school would change if it happens." I looked at him. "Lots would change, yes?"

"Well, Mr. Weatherby, that's not for me to decide, is it?"

"No, it's not," I said.

He paused. "You know, Jason, I've been a teacher here for over thirty years. Chancellor for six."

"Sucks for you, huh? Dealing with a bunch of rich pricks like me."

"What I was alluding to is that politics play a tremendous part in Lambert's history, and in my years here, I've never quite seen an attempt such as this." He paused again, then went on. "To change the very foundation of what Lambert has become is . . . noble."

I gawked. "You're joking, right? You'll have a quarter of this school's parents knocking on your door if I win, and they'll have your head on a platter."

He smiled politely. "Need I remind you that I am merely the steward of policy at Lambert? The charter dictates, not I."

I looked at him. "Why do you talk that way?"

He furrowed his brow.

"Never mind. My bad. What are you saying?"

His eyes met mine. "I'm saying, Mr. Weatherby, that I truly wish you the best of luck. And also that when I spoke to your father this morning, I was under the assumption that he knew of your undertakings here."

I stared at him. "Really?"

He turned away, and as he did, that soft chuckle came again. "Things sometimes evolve in a way they shouldn't, and often-times a person may find friends when there seem to be few around. My apologies for letting your cat out of the bag."

That caught my attention. "You *want* us to win?"

He turned back, grinning. "Sometimes, Mr. Weatherby, rich pricks get tiresome."

Then he was gone, and I felt like a total ass for assuming he was against us. "Huh."

"What?" Brooke said.

"He's stuck in the middle," I laughed. "Just like me."

She grinned. "Did you know he volunteers at a soup kitchen every weekend? My mom told me."

"No, I didn't."

She nodded. "Not everybody is bad, Jason, and nobody is all bad."

CHAPTER TWENTY

"GOT NEWS, JASON."

I looked at Woodsie. Class was out, and he'd caught up to me in the hall. "What?"

He looked away. "Carter called a Chamber meeting today at lunch. You weren't invited."

That didn't surprise me a bit. "What happened?"

"He said you weren't to be trusted, and that you needed to be stopped. I agreed."

"You what?"

He nodded. "Yeah. That's when I told him I was running for secretary of the student council. The same position as Singletary. He'll be my competition."

"Whoa, back up here. You agreed?"

"Yes. I'm running on a different platform than you. A neutral one. I told Carter it was to hedge the Chamber's bet in controlling things if you and Brooke and Elvis make it. I would be the swing vote, because Carter has no intention of Thomas's still being at this school for the election."

"Get to the point, Woods. I'm confused."

"I'm saying we need ears in the Chamber until the election. I'm your ears. And I'm also saying that if Singletary does get the hook, I'll flip."

"You said you couldn't . . ."

"I changed my mind."

"What if you beat Thomas, though?"

"I'll back out due to personal reasons and the next highest vote getter will win the seat, which will be Thomas." He smiled, but it wasn't cheery. More anxious than anything. "It's in the charter."

"This is conspiracy, you know. Not exactly ethical."

He laughed. "I never said I was good, Jason. You've got no say in what I do or don't do, so don't heap guilt on yourself. My decision, my consequences." He eyed me. "Needless to say, it's in my best interests if Singletary wins. I'm counting on you."

I thought about what Brooke had said about bad and good. "You're not bad, Woods."

He smiled. "Life is a fucked-up game. But sometimes you've got to play the game to end the game."

"Yeah, but it's . . ."

"You know fairness doesn't come into play with politics, and you know what will happen if you lose."

I nodded. "Tell me one thing."

He smiled, this time genuine. "Yes, the rumors are true. I'm hung like a horse."

I grunted. "Sicko."

"What one thing, then?"

"Why? Why change your mind?"

He shrugged. "I don't know. Maybe because I can't stand people like Carter."

"Bull."

He stuffed his hands in his pockets. "I told you. I don't know."

I realized that Woodsie was savvy. Incredibly savvy. And that made him dangerous. The most dangerous people in the world were the ones you trusted. "You sure you're on our side?"

"My word."

"I can only believe you, man."

He smiled. "I know. And I can only believe you."

CHAPTER TWENTY-ONE

"WELL, LOOK WHO'S HERE."

I set my keys on the kitchen counter, and my dad stood at the island, his hands splayed on the granite surface. "Hi."

He pointed to my keys, then motioned for me to throw them to him. I did. He put them in his pocket. "You can take a bus from now on."

I stared at him. "Fine with me."

He glowered, his face dropping to a menacing and pissed-off scowl. "Don't test me, son."

"Or what? You'll hit me?"

Silence. He breathed. Then he paced. I'd seen him on TV on the floor of Congress in front of the podium acting the same game. "Let's see. Your wish is to dismantle the only thing that can help you attain success in college. Your wish is to spite me at every turn. Your wish is to throw away everything you've been

119

given." He stopped pacing, staring icicles into me. "That's right, isn't it?"

"This has nothing to do with you, Dad. This is about—"

"THIS HAS EVERYTHING TO DO WITH ME!" he bellowed, slamming his fist on the granite. "I have spent over *a hundred thousand dollars* on your schooling, and *you* have the nerve to tell *me* that I'm not involved?" He came around the counter then, and I stood there, just like I always had. Just like I knew I always would. The jolt of his hands slamming into my chest and grabbing handfuls of my shirt knocked me back against the door. He kept me on my feet, his eyes blazing inches from mine as he shook me. "I am done! Do you hear me? DONE! I won't take your insolence and I will not stand for you making a mockery of this family any longer." He growled, "I will not wake up in the morning regretting you are my son, and you will no longer be the embarrassment of my life. At the end of this semester, you will be attending Rolling Hill Military Academy in Vermont." He stared at me. "Do you understand me, Jason?"

I took a breath, sucking in the heat of his. "No."

His fists tightened on my shirt, his eyes burning into me.

"I'm not going, Dad."

A volcano, he exploded, yanking me forward and slamming me against the back door again. My head snapped back, breaking a pane of glass. As it shattered, he reared a fist back, and I closed my eyes.

"Take your hands from my son."

We both turned our heads, and Mom stood there. No tears, no quivering lip, no hesitation. Just a low and calm voice. Dad's hoarse voice sounded low and dangerous. "Get out of here, Tiffany. Now."

She stood motionless. "You will leave this house right now, Daniel. Go."

"Goddamnit, Tiffany, I don't have to put up . . ."

She opened her phone and punched three numbers. "Yes. My husband is assaulting my son. Yes. That is the correct address. Yes. As quickly as possible." Then she hung up.

Dad let go of me, awestruck. Silence followed as they stared at each other. Then Mom spoke. "I've had enough, Dan."

He stood, staring at the phone, dumbfounded. "Do you know what you've just done to me, Tiffany? I'm a congressman, for God's sake."

"Then act like one," she said.

"You've ruined me."

"You've ruined yourself, and I won't have you ruin my son."

His expression changed then as he regained his composure. He straightened his collar, adjusting his tie. "This won't work. I will not have you destroy me. Either of you. I'm a congressman of the United States of America, and I'll be damned if this will happen."

"You're not above the laws you make, Daniel," she said.

"That's what you don't understand, Tiffany, and that's what Jason will never understand. I am."

"I'm pressing charges."

Three minutes later, my mother proved herself right. She opened the door to two police officers, and five minutes after that, my father was handcuffed and led to a police car.

He spent the night in the jail he'd cut the ribbon on.

CHAPTER TWENTY-TWO

"HEY, SINGLETARY, DID you get your posters done?"

Singletary looked away from me, studying the student parking lot. We stood at the city bus stop across from the school. He held his bus pass in his hand, and the expression on his face was typical; if a smooth slate of stone could somehow have a look of contempt, that would be it. "You think you're smart, don't you?"

I furrowed my brow, as usual in the dark with the guy. "About what?"

He faced me, hair in his eyes, his tone soft. "If you ever come to my home again, I'll come to yours."

"I was trying to warn you."

"I don't need warning."

"Kennedy and Carter. They . . ." I hesitated. "They want you out of the school."

He smiled. "So?"

"So they were planning something to get you out. But things got screwed up."

"And I take it you were a part of things."

"Yes."

He laughed. "So you've become the god who stands up for injustice and wrongdoing by rebelling against *the man*." Humor lit his eyes. "You don't make a good vigilante, Jason. Believe me. You suck at it."

"The system is bent, and I'm doing something about it."

"Let's just get one thing straight, Jason. I don't need you or your causes or anything else, and I don't give a shit about your Chamber and what your grand plan is. This school is exactly like the world, and you aren't going to change anything."

"I can change it."

"No, you'll just become it. That's what people like you don't get. It's like rigged dice. You might roll a four, but it'll always flip back to a six."

"Then why partner up with us?"

"Last I heard, my business was none of yours."

"Something is going on at this school, and—"

He cut me off. "Your dad was on the news. Sounds like a great guy," he said, searching my face. "I'll bet you make a great punching bag."

Even though I had a huge urge to smash him, I didn't. The whole school knew about it, but unlike the others, who politely ignored dirty laundry being publicized, Singletary capitalized on it. The bus pulled up, opening its doors, and I stared at him. "Why are you such a prick?"

A smile, thin and confident, slithered across his face. "Those who believe in fair are the ones who lose," he said, looking at me. "And why I'm a prick is none of your business."

My stomach squirmed. Those words clicked in my brain. "What did you just say?"

He stepped up the stairs, ignoring me, and as the doors closed, I watched him walk down the aisle and sit. He stared at me. No smile, no anger, nothing. Just a flat, dead stare through the dirty window of a dirty bus.

CHAPTER TWENTY-THREE

THOSE WHO BELIEVE in fair are the ones who lose. I spent hours in my room that evening, racking my brains, and finally, I couldn't sit any longer. I snuck downstairs, grabbed my keys, and left.

A chill went down my spine as I stood in the darkness of the Chamber. The silence was complete, eerie, and as I made my way over to a lamp and turned it on, nervous adrenaline pumped through my veins. I squeezed my fists, releasing tension and forcing myself to calm down. But there was a foreboding in me. Something deep and black and as dangerous as the dead stare Thomas Singletary had given me when the bus pulled away. He knew things he shouldn't.

Carter Logan had said those words when we'd talked in this room, and now, as I looked around, my mind reeled. How had he known? I took a breath, then sat in one of the chairs surrounding the table, thinking about everything that had happened in there.

Elvis. The vodka and shot glass. The lead pipe. The twisted words of Carter. Steven Lotus and his fear. Kennedy and his genetic subhuman dysfunction. Woodsie and his strategies. Brooke.

Brooke. Oh God.

I groaned. *You enjoyed the show?* When Singletary had said that, it hadn't registered with me. The show. With Brooke and her blouse. He'd known about it, just like he'd known what Carter said to me. He didn't need warnings from anybody, because he *knew*.

I exhaled, leaning my head back, closing my eyes, and remembering Singletary's file. *He's a hacker.* A computer whiz. Electronics. Technology. He was brilliant. A brilliant, self-made criminal. I'd thought he was immune to fear, some kind of psychotic wrong-side-of-the-tracks mutant, but he wasn't. You can't fear the unknown if you know the unknown, I thought. And that's why I was here. He wasn't magic or psychotic, he was smart.

I opened my eyes, staring at the shadows on the ceiling, then I got up, looking around. The secret was in this room, and I'd find it. I searched then, under the table and chairs, in the lamp shades, between the books on the shelves.

From one corner of the room to the next, I made my way around, and then I saw it. Above the heavy drapes on the far side of the wall. Right at the joint where the ceiling began. A small black dot, no bigger than a dime. Pay dirt.

I dragged a chair over and stood on it, studying the thing. Noting its tiny glass screen, I knew it was a camera, and I swallowed. He'd seen everything, and my mind flashed to Brooke, shame coursing through me. I hopped down, leaving it be, and in another five minutes I'd found the microphone, hidden on the inside edge of a picture frame holding a painting of Thomas Jefferson.

Both were wireless, and I knew enough about wireless to know there had to be a control unit somewhere. I sat down, putting the microphone on the table and thinking. *Singletary knew about the order to break his arm.* I leaned back. Singletary was the one who'd left the pipe with the rose taped to it, because Singletary was the one who attacked Carter. He'd known everything, and the pieces all fell together. All except one question. The big question. Why?

Why would Singletary spy on the Chamber in the first place? He said he didn't care about it, didn't care about anything at Lambert, but he did. He cared a lot. Enough to do this. Enough to . . .

"Out late, huh?"

I jumped, spinning around as my heart pistoned out of control. Singletary stood in the doorway. "What are you doing here?" I asked.

He shrugged, carefully closing the door. "I figured you'd figure it out." He pointed to the microphone on the table. "Looks like you might not be a complete idiot."

I studied him as he walked across the rug and took a seat across the table from me. In the deep cushioned chair, he looked like a twelve-year-old kid, but unlike any twelve-year-old I'd ever met. "You knew the whole time. About the file. Your file. And me."

He nodded. "And by the way, you have *no* idea how much Carter hates you."

I bristled. "And now you're playing these games, and it doesn't bother you that Carter thinks I'm the one doing it."

"Doesn't bother me at all." He smiled. "Actually, I think it's sort of funny."

"I've been the one protecting you, asshole."

"You're pretty crappy at it."

"Tell me what this is about. All of it."

He smirked. "Entertainment."

"Busting an arm is entertainment?"

"Gets boring around here."

"You're full of shit."

"He was going to bust mine, so I figured I'd give him my version of pay it forward." He stared at me, cocking his head, his voice dripping sarcasm. "Is that wrong, Jason? Aren't you doing the same?"

"No, I'm not. You broke his arm. I just want to win an election."

He slouched in the chair, waiting for me to go on, but nothing came. He pointed at my face. "Have you ever hit your dad back?"

"This isn't about my dad."

"Come on, Jase, we're like bros now, right? We can talk."

I clenched my jaw.

He laughed. "Of course you haven't hit the bastard back. But . . . ," he said, eyeing me, "I want to know why you haven't."

"Because."

"Because you're afraid, right? Because *hitting your father* is wrong, and little Jason here is afraid of doing the wrong thing."

I squirmed.

He leaned forward. His voice, sinister and smooth, whispered across the table. "Want to know what happens when you're not afraid anymore, Jason? Want to know what happens when the fear is gone?"

I looked away, rolling my eyes. "Sure. Fire away."

He sat back, and just for a split second, he reminded me of Carter. "When you aren't afraid anymore, you realize that a whole lot of shit that is wrong isn't really wrong. You realize that beating the shit out of your father so badly that he'd never lay another finger on you isn't wrong. It's *justice*."

I smirked. "Yeah. Justice that would land me in juvie."

"What if you weren't afraid of juvie? What if what was *right* was the only thing that mattered?"

I shrugged. "Listen, if people just did what they felt like, everybody would be killing everybody and we'd be living in chaos. That's why we have laws, and you broke the law when you broke his arm." I frowned. "We're civilized. That's what separates us from the animals."

He chuckled. "Dude, you are really messed up in the head, you know that? We're not civilized, we just pretend to be. The predators still kill, man, and it ain't the meth-dealing banger on the corner packing a gun or some middle-class crybaby storming a school with an AK-47. It's the people sitting behind big desks making decisions who kill. They just do it slowly." He stared at me. "Guys like your dad can ruin lives a thousand times easier than guys like me, so don't give me your moral guilt trip about what's civilized and what's not."

"Maybe you're right, but I'm trying to change that. At least here, I am."

"You're not changing anything."

I set my chin. "Yes I am."

"Carter was right. . . ." He paused. "Remember his little speech the first day you were chosen? About the lines of power? About the real purpose behind life being power and control?" He smiled. "He's right, and you can't change it. You can shift it or move it around, but it remains the same in the end. One person controlling another." He grunted. "The little man will always get the shaft, and that's just it. Nada. Nothing more. Your dork friend Elvis is one of them, and you don't like that, so you think you're doing the right thing."

"And you're not one of them?"

He nodded. "I know exactly what I am, but the only difference is that I know the rules are rigged, man, and I reject them. I don't throw the dice anymore. Got my own."

"That's not all true."

He studied me. "You know why I'm poor, Jason?"

I looked away, reminded of my father's private tirades about keeping the poor in their places. The social order.

"Because they need poor people, and they've built a system around it. They need their garbage picked up and their burgers cooked and their lawns mowed and their shit shoveled, and they need to keep us where we are, and you can move things around all you want, but you're never going to change the fact that Carter is right. People love controlling other people."

I flushed, angry because he was so right and so wrong at the same time. "Bullshit. Look at you. You're brilliant. You could get out of it. That's what America is about, right? It's why you're at Lambert." I grunted. "Besides, half the poor people in this country are poor because they like getting free shit from people who work their asses off. Ever heard of welfare?" I sneered.

He laughed, and for the first time, I saw real emotion on his face. Deep, intense, and angry. "Dude, you're so fucking stupid you just buy into it. They *made* it so we *need* it. They made it to keep people on it!" His face went dark then, and his eyes narrowed. "The government has spent seventy years pulling off the biggest lie ever told." He smirked, the hatred in his expression palpable. "You don't make people independent by keeping them dependent, and they know it. Your dad and every other politician keep people dependent for one thing. To own them and their votes. Lives don't matter, man, power does."

I had nothing to say.

He grinned. "That's what I thought. You know how he thinks, huh?"

I looked away. "So you want to change it by breaking Carter's arm. Great. That's retarded."

"I don't want to change anything."

"Then why go after the Chamber?"

"I'm not."

A quiet came over the room as I thought about what he'd just said. "I don't understand you."

He took a breath, exhaling. "I play my own game."

"Against what? Who?" I shook my head. "Carter?"

Silence. After a moment, he rose. "Jason, the only reason I'm helping you with this election deal is because it makes my life easier right now. Other than that, it'd be best if you stayed away from me."

"Why are you at Lambert?"

He nodded at the microphone. "Put that back where you found it, huh?" Then he moved for the door.

"Why'd you tell me this?" I said.

He turned, and in the dim of the lamplit room, his eyes were deep and empty pits. "I don't know." Then he was gone.

CHAPTER TWENTY-FOUR

DAD'S ARREST MADE IT onto *The Late Late Show* as the butt of a few jokes. It must have been a slow news day. As I lay in bed, the clock reading 3:30, I was torn.

My dad wasn't a monster. Singletary might think so, but I knew the decisions he made weren't intended to hurt people. People got hurt in the process, but in the end, I knew more people were helped. *The collective good,* I'd heard my uncle say once. And as my father told me, it took a strong man to make decisions other people were unwilling to make, but just because there was always a loser didn't mean the decision was to be ignored. The weak ignored things.

I groaned, staring at the ceiling. Damned if you do and damned if you don't. I'd heard it a million times, remembering my father's tirades during dinner. Raise taxes and hurt the businessman, lower taxes and hurt the poor. Hit your kid in the face to get him to straighten up, hit him and get arrested. There was always the one who got screwed, no matter what. But Singletary made me think that maybe down beneath it all, the game *was* rigged, and maybe no one person could change a system built to protect itself. My father was a part of that system and, I knew, I was, too. We all were.

Which made me think of my face. I sat up, rubbing my eyes. I knew Dad cared about me, but I also knew that life hadn't turned out the way he'd wanted. I hadn't turned out the way he'd wanted, and I never would, either. He was screwed up, sure, and his dad hit him when he was growing up, but I understood. He wanted the all-star son and he got the all-star reject.

I also knew that thousands of husbands and fathers were arrested each day for abuse in this country, but they weren't plastered all over the news. There was no circus for them and no media hype, but for my dad, there was, and it was as wrong as his hitting me in the first place. Maybe Singletary knew something about justice that I didn't, but I couldn't bring myself to hate because of it. I loved my dad, and there was no right or wrong in that. It just was.

I got out of bed and padded downstairs. Dad had posted bail and was staying at a hotel somewhere, but I couldn't shake the feeling that he was here, lurking over my shoulder, waiting to unload on me.

I opened the fridge, taking the milk out and swigging when I heard footsteps across the hardwood of the dining room. I froze for an instant before my mom came around the corner. In the dimness of the kitchen, she looked tired. Worn. She sat on a stool at the island, arranging her robe. "I couldn't sleep, either."

I put the cap on the milk. "Yeah."

"I'm sorry about this, Jason."

"Why?"

"Because this is my fault."

"You didn't hit me."

"I know, but you were right the other morning. I should have never allowed it to happen the first time. I never should have been silent."

I swallowed milk phlegm, clearing my throat. "What's going to happen?"

"I don't know."

"Can I ask you a question?"

"Of course. Anything."

"Do you think he's bad? I mean, what he does? All the decisions he makes and people he affects?"

She took a breath. "Are you talking about what you're doing at Lambert?"

"Sort of. I'm just screwed up right now." I studied the calendar on the fridge. "You think the world is like Lambert? That it's all just a setup? All power and money and control?"

She smiled. "So what you're really asking is if you are turning into your father."

"Yeah, I guess."

She stood, walking over and hugging my shoulders from behind. "The only thing I know for sure is that I think you are doing the right thing, Jason."

"Why can't Dad be proud of me?" I looked to the floor. "I screw up all the time, Mom. Nothing ever works with him. I can even run for a stinking position just like him and he doesn't like it."

She patted my shoulder. "In a way, I think your father may feel as if you are attacking him by trying to change Lambert, but that's his issue to deal with." She walked around me, raising my chin with her finger. "I'm proud of you for this, Jason. It takes courage, and in that way, you *are* just like your father."

"Do you love him?"

She paused. "Yes, I do. He's a good man, and I know you don't really think so at this time, but he's tried to help a lot of people in his life, and he's been a good husband and father." She looked away, smiling. "His first term in office, Jason, you should have known him. He was so . . . excited to do good. To make a difference. And he has. But he's lost track of things as the years have gone by." She looked up. "Do you understand that?"

"I understand I'll never be what he wants."

She nodded. "You should be who you are, not what other people want. And that includes your father."

I thought about it, and I realized that what I wanted was for all of this to never have happened. I wished it would just go away. I wished my dad would be like my mom said he used to be. Like the dad I remembered when I was little. "I want him to love me."

She stood. "He does."

"Maybe deep down, but . . ." I held back, my eyes burning.

"But nothing. He loves you, Jason, but he needs to come to terms with you."

"Yeah, because I'm a screwup."

"No. Because you're a different person. You think differently, and your father is used to battling those who think differently."

"Politics as usual."

"Yes, it is. And it's his nature."

"Winners and losers and suckers."

She hugged me again. "You're a winner."

I laughed. "Thanks."

She ruffled my hair. "Everything will turn out. You'll see."

"Are you divorcing him?"

"No, I'm not. I love him and I'm willing to help him if he wants help. It will be up to him, because I've set my terms."

CHAPTER TWENTY-FIVE

"WE'RE AT AN IMPASSE here, Jason."

I glanced again at the cast on his arm. When I'd broken my arm two years ago, within days I'd had a dozen signatures on it from friends. Carter's was white. Pristine, blank, and as empty as the obsidian pools looking at me. "An impasse?"

He closed my gym-locker door. The place was empty. Silent but for the dripping echo of a leaky showerhead. He took a breath. "Do you really want to see this situation escalate?"

"I didn't break your arm, and no, I don't want to see it escalate."

He shook his head. "I don't think you did. I'm talking about the Leadership Group. The Chamber. This idiotic plan of yours to overthrow it."

"It's wrong."

He smiled. "So there we are. You want something, and I want something."

"You're scared I'll win, aren't you?"

He rolled his eyes. "Listen, Jason, it's no secret I can't stand you. I hate your guts, actually. I hate who you are and what you are and why I had to put you in the Chamber. But we both need something the other can give."

"I don't need anything from you."

He took his phone from his pocket. "Yes, you do."

I studied him. "Why do you care so much about this, Carter? You're gone at the end of the year. Lambert will be history."

He smiled again. "I care because you think you're better than me, but you're not."

"This is about the school, Carter. Not you."

He shrugged. "I'm offering a compromise."

"And the terms?"

He shrugged again. "Make him stop, and I won't stand in your way."

I stared. "Who?"

He held his cast up. "Singletary." He paused. "Talk to him, make him stop, get rid of him—out of this school, gone wherever—and you can have your little election and do whatever you want with the Chamber. Complete and total control."

"You think Singletary is the one hassling you?"

"Yes, I do. And you are helping him."

I thought about it. "I don't know what you're talking about."

"I'm not an idiot. I looked at the roster of candidates. Singletary pulled into the race."

"So?"

"So the only logical conclusion is that he's in with you. You told him about the file, and he's paying me back."

"I'm not helping him do anything."

139

His expression darkened. "Get rid of him, Jason."

"Why? Just like you said, without him we won't have a majority, and if you think I'll trust you for a minute, you're more insane than you already are. I'm going to beat you, Carter, and there's nothing you can do about it. So no, we're not at an impasse. You have a problem and it's not mine."

"I'll give you one last chance here. Get rid of him and I promise on everything I am that you will win. I can make it happen. I can give you the majority without him." He paused. "And by the way, have you thought about Elvis? The letter he needs to get into his school?"

"He doesn't want it."

"Don't fool yourself, and don't think for a minute that he doesn't hate you for dragging him into something that will dismantle the only hope he has for making his life anything other than a big pile of shit." He studied me. "Do you understand what you did to him? You and I have it easy. People like him don't. They have nothing, and you don't give a crap about it, do you? You ruined him."

I stared.

"As the Chamber president, I'm the only one who can write the letter, Jason. And I'll do it if you work with me. I'll write the letter the day of the elections."

"You're a bastard."

"And you're killing your best friend's chance at a good life."

"I don't need you."

He flipped open his phone, then looked at me. "Elvis needs me, though."

I clenched my teeth. "I'm not scared of you."

He dialed his phone, talking into it. "Five minutes," he said, finally, then closed the phone and met my eyes. "You should be scared of me."

I looked at him.

His voice cut through the silence. "You crossed me, Jason, and you shouldn't have."

I shook my head. "Why can't you just give it up?"

"That's the difference between you and me, Jason. You have boundaries," he said, gesturing at his phone, "and I don't."

I pointed to the phone in his hand. "Who was that?"

His eyes met mine. "Time is short, so I'll be blunt. Kennedy has your friend Elvis pinned down in an abandoned warehouse." He paused. "It seems you left him a note to meet you there to talk . . . election strategy." The hint of a smile touched his lips. "Unless you agree to our deal, the brute is going to break both of his arms." He held up his cast. "A kind of tit for tat, just twice the pain. I'm sure your friend Singletary understands the concept."

I lunged at him, slamming him against the bank of lockers. "I swear to God if you . . ."

He remained calm. "Make your mind up, Jason."

"You'll face charges. Both of you."

"You are aware of who my father is, correct? He might be a drunk asshole, but he has so many friends on the bench it's ridiculous. And Kennedy's father? You really think charges would hold up?"

"Yes. I'd make sure of it."

"You can't." He paused. "Do you think that two broken arms are worth changing your life, Jason?"

"No."

"As I said. We're different than Elvis. He won't press charges if I promise him the letter. He may have refused it before, but that was pride. For his father. This is different. Besides, there will be no witnesses. Kennedy's word against a trash collector's son. He'll know it, too." He tapped the side of his head with his finger. "Be smart here, Jason. Come on."

"Don't do this, Carter."

"I will do it, and I'll do more unless we have some cooperation." He glanced at his watch. "You have less than three minutes."

I let him go, yanking my phone from my pocket and calling Elvis. It rang five times before the connection came through. "Elvis, where are you?"

"Hey, Jason! Kennedy here. Your buddy and I are just about to have a little party. You're missing it."

I swallowed, looking at the floor, no words coming to me. I closed the phone. "This is insane."

He looked at his watch. "Two minutes, Jason."

"You'll go to jail for this. There's no way you could get out of it."

"Make up your mind."

Panic swept through me, and I knew he was obsessed. He *didn't* have boundaries. "Okay."

He growled, "You'll get rid of him, pay him off, hurt him, do whatever is necessary, right?"

"Yes."

"You'll denounce his candidacy as part of your platform." ·

I breathed.

"Answer me."

"Yes."

He called. "Party is canceled, Kennedy. Sorry to spoil your fun." He closed the phone, then slipped it into his pocket. "Your friend is at 5205 North Market Street." He nodded. "You might want to hop on over and let him loose."

I turned to leave.

"Jason?" he called. I faced him, and as he stood there, something in his eyes struck me. Fear. He nodded. "I just wanted to tell you you'll regret it if you break your word."

CHAPTER TWENTY-SIX

DRIED BLOOD CAKED his mouth, and a baseball bat lay next to him. A bolt of dread shot through me. "Did he . . ."

"No. Just punched me for the fun of it."

I struggled with the rope around the legs of the desk. "This has gone too far," I said. He said nothing. Minutes passed before I finally freed him. He sat there, rubbing his wrists, and I stood across from him. "This is all my fault."

"Pretty much, yeah."

I rolled my eyes, staring at the ceiling. "Thanks."

"Well, it is. I didn't say that was bad, though."

"It is bad."

He swallowed, joining me in concentrating on the rafters. "He was going to do it, you know?"

"Kennedy?"

"Yeah. He *wanted* to. I could tell. He was excited. I think he had a boner."

I cleared my throat, thinking.

"It doesn't matter anymore, because we're done. The whole thing is off."

"I'm not done."

I looked at him. "What?"

He sighed. "When I was standing in the Chamber that day, I realized something, Jason. The world shouldn't be this way, and I'm not quitting. I'm done being the guy tied to a desk in an abandoned building."

"Carter is crazy, Elvis. Insane."

He shrugged. "I've got nothing to lose."

We sat in silence for a while, in agony over our options. "Tell me the truth?" I said, finally.

"About what?"

"Why are you running with me?"

"Because it's right."

I shook my head. "You're giving up Pilkney for it."

He smiled. "Yeah, I am."

"Why?"

"I told you. This is right."

"I can't let you do that. I'm getting you the letter."

"No."

I shifted. "You're making this really hard."

"Maybe."

"If none of this was happening, you'd be going there. That's wrong, Elvis. Way wrong."

"That's life."

Moments passed, the dusty room silent. "So what now?" I said.

"So we keep on with what we're doing," he laughed. "And I'll carry pepper spray from now on."

"We can bail any time."

"We can beat him, Jason."

I stood, nodding even as my insides twisted and churned. "Ride home?"

"Sure. I'm helping my mom size dresses."

"Size dresses?"

"Yeah. I have to wear them while she measures."

"You are weird, you know that?"

He clucked. "Yeah, I know. I just have to think of an excuse for a bloody mouth. You can help me with that."

CHAPTER TWENTY-SEVEN

I DIDN'T REALLY feel like James Bond or Inspector Gadget as I sat on the curb across the street from Thomas Singletary's apartment building. More like a fish out of the aquarium that was my life. I'd ditched my car in the parking lot of a Rite Aid a mile up the hill, and I'd walked, now sitting on the curb for the last hour waiting for him to show himself. I read my watch. Nine-thirty-five.

I shivered, glancing up and down the dark street, then focused on the building entrance. I could have just gone in and knocked, but I didn't. It was like a breach of territory, and his warning about visiting his apartment kept me back. Courtesy, I thought, chuckling at what a liar I was.

I didn't knock on his door because I was frightened to. Something about Thomas Singletary scared the living shit out of me.

"Homeless now?"

I started, looking to my left, and of course, like a silent sentinel, Thomas was next to a garbage can chained to a NO PARKING signpost. I stood. "No."

He smiled. "You shouldn't be in this neighborhood. You might get hurt."

I looked around. "Not that bad."

He laughed this time. "You are so full of shit."

"I can take care of myself."

"There were fourteen murders in this city last year. Nine of them were committed within ten blocks of here." He studied me, humor in his eyes. "How many in your neighborhood?"

"I don't know."

"Bullshit."

"Fine. None."

He nodded. "Why are you here?"

"This is going too far."

"What is?"

I sighed. "This crap with the Chamber and Carter."

He shrugged. "Define *too far.*"

I clenched my teeth. "Too far is almost having my friend's arms broken, you asshole. It's not just me and you anymore."

"Key word *almost.* It didn't happen."

I stared at him. "You knew about it?"

"Duh. Remember the Chamber? Those little electronic things you found? Eyes and ears."

"And you let it happen."

"I've explained myself enough. You should know by now I roll my own dice."

"He doesn't have anything to do with this, and you're standing there telling me it wouldn't bother you a bit to see the guy at school tomorrow with both his arms in casts." I shook my head. "You're causing all of this."

"I didn't cause anything. I told you from the beginning to stay out of things, but you didn't, so if you want to blame anybody, look in the mirror."

I set my jaw, pissed off. "I told Carter it was you," I lied.

"I figured you would."

"Yeah, I did. And now I'm telling you to stop."

"Or what?"

I was at my wit's end. Or what? Or nothing. I couldn't make anybody stop anything. "Why are you after Carter?"

"My business, not yours."

"No, it *is* my business, because Carter is going to keep coming after me if I don't get you to stop. And that means he'll go after Elvis and Brooke and anybody else who gets in the way."

He smiled. "Then it looks like you have a problem."

"No, it means you have a problem. I'll take you out before they get hurt, Thomas. I will."

"You'll take me out, huh?" He stepped closer. "I own you, motherfucker."

I stepped up to him. "Don't threaten me."

"You going to hit me now, big boy? You think that will get you out of this mess?"

A moment passed. "Who are you?" I said.

"Nobody you'd ever want to know."

I stepped back, utterly frustrated. "Carter is scared shitless of you, and Kennedy won't touch you. Why?"

"Now you're getting it. Carter is scared of me because he has no control over me, and Kennedy, well, let's just say Kennedy is a pill popper with a . . . confidential rehab file. He and I struck a deal. Sort of like a 'don't ask, don't tell' thing."

"Pills? How'd you find out?"

He laughed. "God, you really are stupid. Come on, Jason, get with it. You read my file. I'm a hacker. That's what I do. I found out who his psych doctor was and took a spin through his file system."

Unease filled me as I realized this went further than anything I knew. "You hacked your grade records to get into Lambert, didn't you?"

"D'oh. Now I let it out." He smirked. "Don't tell anybody, okay? I wouldn't want to be embarrassed if all my friends found out I wasn't brilliant."

"Why come to Lambert in the first place?"

He turned away. "We're done talking."

I stared at his back, calling after him, "What are you going to do?"

His only answer was a middle finger thrown my way.

CHAPTER TWENTY-EIGHT

"I'M GOING TO PUKE."

I looked at Elvis. He wore a suit and tie, and had his hair combed, greased, and parted like a kid stuck forever in the fifties. "Your mom did your hair, huh?"

He nodded, adjusting his coat. His hands shook. "She took me to Sears last night and got the suit. She usually makes everything, but she told me this was special."

"They're cool, aren't they?"

"My parents? Yeah."

We stood behind the stage curtain with the other candidates, readying ourselves for campaign speeches. The auditorium was packed. We'd worked on individual campaign ads in the audio/visual room for the last two days, too, and all candidates would have theirs played on the projector screen after giving their speeches.

With voting immediately following, this would be the big moment. Elvis, myself, and Brooke were basically campaigning as a team, and we'd blended our speeches, even combining our video. Today would also be the day I would declare Singletary as a candidate running on our platform, and that a vote for him was a vote for us.

Either way, the lines of battle would be clearly drawn, then.

Woodsie sat in a chair to the side, nonchalant as usual. I walked over to him, nodding. "Woods."

"Hey, Jason."

"You ready?"

"Sure."

I breathed, calming myself. "Carter gave me an ultimatum."

Woodsie nodded. "I know."

Silence followed, and rage built in me. "You knew Kennedy was going to do it?"

"No. Carter called a meeting last night. Explained the situation." He swallowed, and a moment passed. "So you're in a big mess."

"Yeah."

He furrowed his brow. "Are you lying to Carter, or did you cut a real deal with him about Singletary?"

"I don't know."

"Well, you'd better know soon, because the guy is in psycho mode."

"What did he say? Does he believe me?"

"Carter never believes anybody."

"I don't know what to do."

He stood. "You know your answer, Jason. You just don't want to face it."

"Maybe."

He looked across the room, to where Brooke and Elvis stood. "He could be the next Einstein."

"You love rubbing things in."

He shrugged. "Just the truth."

"I need that letter for him."

"You could forge one."

"No. I might stoop low, but not that low."

"So it comes down to Singletary, who's about as crazy as Carter, or Elvis, who doesn't have anything to do with this."

Silence.

He went on. "Jason, if you dump Singletary, I can fill his spot. No harm done, then."

"I know."

He groaned. "Oh no."

"What?" I said.

"I've heard that in your voice before."

"What?"

"You were about to say that my taking Singletary's place wasn't the point, weren't you?"

"Yes. Because it's not the point. Carter would win, and besides, I'm not going to get Singletary kicked out of Lambert."

"But with me on the council it wouldn't matter."

"Yes, it would. To me."

He eyed me. "Crap. You like Singletary, don't you?"

"No. He's just . . . there's something about the guy. Believe me, he's just about as psycho as Carter, but different."

He rocked on his heels. "You do know that the whole school knows about Singletary joining the race, right?"

I glanced at him.

He nodded. "Word got out."

"Who?"

"Me," he said.

I deflated. "Why?"

"Well, after Elvis almost had his arms broken and you and Carter came to 'terms' about Singletary, I thought a leak would hedge things so that I wouldn't win and have to decline." He swallowed, looking across the auditorium. "And it did hedge things without getting anybody hurt by Carter. But now you've got every person in the place waiting for the messiah to deliver his message."

"Thanks. Now if I don't do it, the whole school will hate me."

He laughed, nodding at the growing crowd. "Pretty much."

"I'm screwed."

"Yeah."

I shook my head. "Did Carter say why he's bombing to get Singletary out? I just can't figure out how it all started."

"Does there need to be a reason?"

I shrugged. "True."

He slid me a look. "I wonder how the kid knew about the order to break his arm."

"He knows a lot," I said.

"You tell him?"

"No. But I'd watch what you say in the Chamber."

As the auditorium filled and the lights dimmed, we sat on the stage in metal chairs, all of us lined up like monkeys in a row. One chair remained empty. Thomas Singletary would be the surprise announcement of the day. Or was supposed to have been. I couldn't help shuddering at the idea of it. Brooke had thought

154

it up and I'd agreed. It would add mystery, excitement, and flavor to the election. A coup, she'd said, laughing. Now it would be my demise, and my chest tightened as I thought about what I should do.

Mr. Belmont, my old English teacher, stepped up to the microphone. Polished and smooth, his hands resting on each side of the podium like a preacher's, he began with a broad grin. "Well, here we are. The Lambert elections. Once again, we will be deciding who is best suited to lead us into the future, and today we'll be greeted with each candidate's vision of that future. And after we've seen what these fine speakers can offer, you'll be excused to vote." He swept his arm over us. The auditorium burst with applause. He went on, explaining how the afternoon would proceed, and asking that applause be held until each candidate was finished with the video presentation. Then he announced the first candidate, Lawrence Wolke, who was running for treasurer. His mother was the senior vice president of LoCorp, the largest defense contractor in the state.

As he took the podium, he cleared his throat and began. I didn't hear a word. The pimply-faced kid was nice enough, but I was like a little boy listening to a lecture, my mind on Singletary and Carter and Elvis. Woodside had taken the situation and sharpened it to a razor's edge, and it sliced my insides apart like a whirlwind ninja on a rampage. Elvis was the only one with no blood on his hands, but he was the one who could pay the biggest price.

A tense anticipation hung over the audience as each candidate stepped up to the podium. The reaction to each video presentation, no matter how well done, was subdued and expectant. Almost like a calm before the storm.

Sitting on the stage with everybody, a movement at the edge of the curtain caught my eye. A freshman silently handed a folded piece of paper to Vivica Peterson, who sat closest to the curtain and was running against Elvis for treasurer. The frosh whispered in her ear; she nodded, then passed the paper to the next person. It made its way down to me. My name was written on it.

As the candidate preceding us droned on about budgets and cost-effective measures that would save the school money while "enhancing the viable academic programs that are a treasure to Lambert," I opened up the paper. It read:

Brooke looks very nice today.
Remember the deal.

I took a deep breath, studying the words, then folded it up. A chill ran through me. I raised my eyes to the crowd, scanning the rows. At the very back, standing and leaning against the right-side entrance, was Carter, his pose laconic, but his eyes burning into me through the dimness. Even at this distance, his intensity scared the living crap out of me.

I tore my stare from him and saw Kennedy sitting next to Steven Lotus in the third row. He smiled, blew me a kiss, then nodded to Brooke as he fluttered his tongue in a grotesque message that was as clear as the note.

I wanted to run. To hide. And I had minutes to decide who I would betray. Minutes to find a way out of this trap. I slid my hand to Brooke, sitting next to me, taking her hand in mine and squeezing. She squeezed back, keeping her eyes forward. "Nervous?" she whispered.

I squeezed her hand again as the video presentation ended and Mr. Belmont rose to introduce me as a candidate for president. As he finished and gestured my way, I took a breath and rose, walking to the podium. Woodsie shook my hand as I passed, whispering in my ear, "Humpty Dumpty sat on a wall . . ."

I took the podium, my back sweaty from the seat and my legs weak. I grasped the sides of the wood-veneered lectern with trembling fingers, my mind racing, my ribs clutching my heart like a vise. I stood in a sound vacuum; not a peep could be heard as the student body stared at me, waiting. Then I saw him.

My dad stood at one of the doors.

I couldn't talk. I wanted to scream, but I couldn't do that, either. I was frozen. The moment of truth had come and there was no truth. There was no right or wrong, only consequences, and it was up to me to decide them. I realized in that moment that my father was correct about one thing. Most people would rather have others make the important decisions. Decisions where choice equaled pain for one and victory for another.

I cleared my throat. "My name is Jason Weatherby, and I'm running for student council president," I said, desperately trying to quell the shake in my voice. Expectant looks from the auditorium. God, I lived in a fishbowl, and the world was gawking at me. I lowered my head, taking a moment, then raised my chin. "The United States of America was founded on the principles of freedom, liberty, and choice. Our forefathers declared that our government be run by the people and for the people, and since then, those principles have carried us through over two hundred years of struggle. It has also shown our people that the fundamental ideals of being a republic rely upon the strength, courage, and integrity of the leaders we elect. But our leaders are put to a task where the decisions they make, while helping some, will hurt others, and the gauge of how well they've made those decisions rests within the people who elect them. The voters." I stopped, scanning the crowd before going on.

"I was recently told that there are lines of power in this country. From the highest level to the lowest, there is an order that determines why we live the way we do, why we are the way we are, and how we do the things we do. It's an incredibly powerful and unseen force, but it's there, and I'm standing here today telling you that it *should* be there. Those lines are needed, because otherwise we'd have chaos. But the lines of power should begin with the people, end with the people, and be bound by the truth. And at this school, those lines of power aren't. They begin in a room called the Chamber, and those decisions are made by one person." I stopped, taking a breath before going on.

"And that one person, the so-called president of the Chamber of Five, is not elected. He's chosen. He's chosen based on lines of power that are corrupt and do nothing but weaken who we are. That is not a republic, nor does it fit within the guidelines of democracy. It is a dictatorship. And if elected, I am going to do everything I can to abolish the Chamber with a majority vote, as the Lambert School for the Gifted student charter dictates any student organization can be. Further, Youth Leadership Group membership will be dictated by the student council, and the decisions for membership will be based solely on what this school was founded for: academic excellence."

The auditorium erupted in thunderous applause, and I saw my father step back, out of the room. I sighed, looking across the auditorium toward Carter, who stood as before, his pose indifferent and relaxed, but his face hard. He nodded slowly. Now was the time for decisions.

I waited for the applause to die down, and as I did, I glanced at Brooke. She beamed as she clapped, her eyes meeting mine, and I felt like a psychic looking into the face of a person doomed. I swiveled my head back to the crowd.

"For the students at Lambert who want those lines of power put back where they should be, I need help, and for that, I'd like to introduce my running mates, the candidates who will allow us to achieve our goal." I then went on to introduce Brooke, who joined me at the podium and gave a short speech about what she would do as vice president, including streamlining the process of getting budgetary approval for academic clubs and extracurricular programs that benefit the community.

Next came Elvis. He loped up to the podium, and I stepped aside, allowing him the microphone. He bobbed his head. "Hi. Uh, I'm Elvis." A long moment passed, the audience expectant, silent, waiting. He stared out over them as if expecting something to happen. I cleared my throat, then nudged him. Startled, he lowered his head to the microphone, banging his nose against it. "Um, this school sort of sucks the way it is now. Let's, uh, make it different. Thank you."

I smiled as the audience burst into applause. Hoots and hollers followed, with a chant of "ELVIS!!!" subsiding when I took the microphone. "The last candidate on our ticket," I said, my eyes finding Carter, "is Thomas Singletary."

Silence.

I took a breath. "As a freshman, Thomas has come to understand that we share a common goal, and that goal is to change this school. To make it fair, equal, and representative of all of us. So without any further ado, I'd like to introduce him to you." I found him in the crowd and motioned for him to join us. He hesitated, then stood and made his way down the aisle and up onto the stage. I stepped aside, allowing him to take the podium.

Shorter than Elvis, he bent the microphone down. He took a second, glanced at me with those dead eyes, and began. "You're all clowns."

I shuddered.

He went on, shaking his head. Then he pointed, one by one, to Kennedy, Carter, Woodsie, and Lotus. "My dad used to say every victim deserves being a victim because he doesn't have the nuts to figure out how to stop being a victim. Every single one of you is a victim to these scumbags, and honestly, I don't care if you change it. I don't give a crap if you vote for me or Jason or his little girlfriend or the geek of the week, because you get what you deserve. So if you want to change it, go ahead. If not, don't complain. That's all." He then stepped away, standing straight, his eyes burrowing into Carter at the back of the auditorium.

I melted inside, wondering if he'd just pissed off the people who could make this happen. I stepped past him toward the microphone. "You definitely have a way with words," I whispered.

"Play the video," he said.

I raised the microphone. "Thomas has a way of cutting to the chase, eh?" I said, hoping for a reaction and getting random

160

applause. "Now, without interruption, I'd like to show you our video montage," I continued, then signaled up to the control room before we took our seats, turning to watch. The lights dimmed as the screen above us lit up.

Before the first images appeared, a voice came over the speakers. Soft, sardonic, full of arrogance, and recognizable, it began. "I'll show them who rules this school."

Brooke and Elvis both turned to me, questions in their eyes. I took a breath. Carter. The voice was that of Carter. On our video. Panic swept through me as I searched the auditorium for him. Singletary was orchestrating the ultimate payback, and I could do nothing about it.

I found Carter, but in the dim light I couldn't see his expression. I turned back to the front, where the screen faded into a scene. The crowd went silent as an incredibly clear picture of the Chamber came into focus, the camera peering down on the table. Carter and Kennedy lounged in the chairs. "You know why I am what I am?" Carter said. "Because people are sheep, and sheep need to be herded."

The scene switched then. Carter speaking again, this time to Steven Lotus. "You know why we don't have that many welfare scum here, Lotus? Genetics. Stupid breeds stupid."

Mr. Belmont sprinted for the control room.

The scene flicked again, this time Kennedy speaking. "Yeah, I took care of it, Carter." Kennedy guffawed. "You should have seen the bitch when I told her she would be running on our platform. She said no at first, but when I brought up the fact that I'd *really* enjoy myself with her if she didn't, there wasn't a problem."

I looked down the row of candidates, my stomach churning

as I watched Vivica, running against Elvis, cringing and shrinking in her seat.

The sound bites went on, changing every few seconds as Mr. Belmont could be heard banging on the control-room door. Carter scathed the chancellor, teachers, the administration, everything and anything, as the audience gaped silently at the cruelty. They heard Carter order the breaking of Singletary's arm. They heard bits of wicked and cruel conversations about various girls in the school who Carter thought "attractive." All of them only seconds long, carefully edited bytes of destruction, and enough to make me sick. All caught on the surveillance camera.

I looked back to Carter, but he was gone. The chancellor ghost stood completely still, his hands clasped before him, staring at me. He knew there was no stopping what was happening, but from the expression on his face, I was sure there would be hell to pay. I looked at Thomas, and he sat, stone-faced. After the most damaging three minutes of video I'd ever seen, and with the DVD still rolling scenes of Brooke about to be forced to take her shirt off in the Chamber, the lights went up and the stage curtain was swept in front of the screen as Carter spoke to Lotus about being a whore.

I leaned toward Thomas. "You just got me killed."

He stared ahead. "You wanted to be elected. You got it."

"We had this in the bag. You were going to get your wish. Carter was already on the way out."

He stood as the audience, stunned, began filing from the auditorium to the booming voice of Mr. Belmont ordering everybody back to class. "Your wishes aren't mine, Jason. I told you that." Then Thomas turned, and was met by Brooke's open hand slapping his face. Hard. Harder than she'd slapped me.

She fumed. "You dirty little bastard!"

He touched his lip, then straightened. "I didn't whore myself out. You did." Then he walked away.

I stood as Brooke turned and glared at me. "I swear to God if you had *anything* to do with this, I will kill you!" She stomped forward, jabbing a finger in my face.

CHAPTER TWENTY-NINE

A HALF HOUR LATER, Elvis, Brooke, Thomas, and I sat in the chancellor's office as the voting went on. Patterson didn't speak as his eyes roamed from face to face. His nose hairs were so long they blended with his mustache. Deep-set sockets locked on mine. "I am demanding that if you win this race, you resign immediately, Mr. Weatherby. You've created quite a spectacle."

I shifted in my seat.

"*He* made the spectacle?" Thomas said, surprising us all.

The chancellor paused. "Excuse me?"

"You said he caused a spectacle."

He nodded. "He has. The school is in an uproar, and this behavior is unacceptable by any student at Lambert." He looked at me. "I thought you to be different than this, Mr. Weatherby."

Thomas cut in. "He didn't do anything."

"Who did, then? You?" the chancellor questioned.

Thomas shook his head. "Well, by the looks of the video, Carter did."

The chancellor frowned. "I'm dealing with you right now, Mr. Singletary. You and your friends."

Thomas sat forward. "You saw the video," he said, staring at the chancellor. "You saw it, and *we're* sitting here?"

"As I said, I am dealing with *you*."

Thomas's face flushed in anger. "Are you retarded?"

He cleared his throat. "That, Mr. Singletary, just landed you in detention for one week," he said, scribbling on a pad of paper.

Brooke cut in. "Thomas is right. What about Carter? Isn't what he's done more important than everybody seeing what he's done?"

"I will be speaking with Carter Logan separately, and I can assure you that his behavior will be fully investigated."

Thomas laughed, shaking his head.

The chancellor picked his pen up again. "You find something humorous?"

"You're a joke."

His voice lowered. "This is *not* a laughing matter. Lambert does not and *will* not tolerate this disruption, and I will not tolerate your attitude."

Thomas sat back, leveling a stare at him. "You're a *fucking* joke, and this school is a joke."

He scribbled. "Another week."

Thomas turned to me. "See, Jason? I told you. Mr. Jerkoff here can stand there and watch what Carter does to people, and what happens? Nothing. That ass and his drunk father get a free pass while we sit in here and listen to this puppet tell us what's right and what's wrong."

"You just earned yourself a week suspension, Thomas," Chancellor Patterson said. "And you are hovering toward—"

"You can take your suspension and shove it up your ass."

"You are hovering near an expulsion, Thomas," he went on. "I would suggest you calm down immediately. Now, Jason"—he looked at me—"why did you make that video? You should know better than anyone in this room that there are proper channels to go through to bring a greivance or complaint against another student."

I took a breath, and my stomach shriveled. Thomas was right. He'd been right all along. Nothing would ever change. "You saw the video, sir, but *we're* here. Not Carter. It doesn't make sense."

"Answer me."

Thomas snorted. "Come on, Jason, answer him. Why did you make the video?"

I swallowed, taking a breath. "I didn't."

He looked at me, narrowing his eyes. "Who did?"

Silence. Then Thomas spoke. "I did."

The chancellor sat back, clasping his hands across his belly. "You recorded private conversations in the Chamber, made the video, and replaced it with the original that was to be played this afternoon?"

Thomas smiled, and it was a smile that said something had popped in him. A line had been crossed, and Chancellor Patterson had no idea what he was dealing with. This was the Thomas Singletary I knew. "Yep. I also broke his arm. You should have heard it snap."

Patterson nodded. "I will be petitioning the board for your removal from this school. Your mother will be hearing from me, and the authorities will be contacted concerning your admission of breaking Carter Logan's arm. I'm sure charges will be pressed."

Thomas grimaced with contempt. "You're a tool."

He looked away. "Dismissed."

Thomas flipped him the finger. "You don't tell me what to do. Nobody does."

The chancellor picked up the phone. "I'm taking that as a threat."

Thomas stood. "Think I care what you think?" He pointed to the phone. "Go ahead. Call the police."

A moment passed, then the chancellor set the phone down. His eyes met Thomas's. "I'd like to solve this in a civilized manner. Please sit down, Mr. Singletary."

Thomas stared. "I'd like to know if you've called the police on Carter. He broke several laws. You saw him ordering Kennedy to break my arm. You also heard Kennedy reporting to Carter about threatening a student with rape unless she did what they wanted."

He hesitated. "That is my concern, not yours. I've explained that I will be looking into the video."

Thomas smirked. "I'll tell you what will happen. You'll get a call from his drunk-ass father, then his grandfather, and this will all go away." He shook his head, looking at me. "You almost changed my mind, Jason. You were wrong, man. There's no justice, just like I said. Only payback." He nodded to the chancellor. "Guys like this need to meet the heavy end of a baseball bat. It's the only way," he said, standing.

The chancellor stood. "I just heard another threat, Mr.

Singletary." He picked up the phone again, keeping his eyes on Thomas. "Sit down right now. I'm calling security, then the police, and you will remain here until they arrive. You are dangerous."

Thomas smiled, the wicked slit of his mouth hard and thin. "Or what?"

He dialed. "Yes, send security to my office immediately and call the police."

I was speechless, because deep down inside, I knew Thomas was right. I'd been on the receiving end of things just like Carter, and I'd never thought about the other side. My father had been right all along, too. Life wasn't what you did, it was who you were, and I'd just seen it happen in the most horrible way.

He hung up. "You will be detained until the police arrive. Sit down."

Thomas took a step toward the chancellor, balling his hand into a fist. He slammed it down on the desk, scattering a pen and bouncing a paperweight. "OR WHAT?"

Fear flooded into Chancellor Patterson's eyes, and his face drained of color. Silence.

I stood. "Don't, Thomas. Just leave. Go."

Thomas nodded, his whole being exuding quiet and dangerous rage. "That's what I thought," he said, contempt oozing from him. Then he turned. As he walked past me, he bent, whispering in my ear, "It ends now. Stay away." Then he was gone, out the door and running down the hall.

The chancellor took a moment, staring at the open door, then regained his composure. "You are all dismissed until further notice."

Elvis spoke. "What about the election? You said . . ."

The chancellor cleared his throat. "I am taking Mr. Single-tary's admission into consideration. As of now, the three of you are valid candidates. But," he said, "that may change depending on circumstances. I will be contacting each of your parents for further discussion on the matter."

CHAPTER THIRTY

AT TWO-FIFTEEN, in the middle of fifth period, the intercom crackled, and every head in the room looked up at the old box above the door. Since leaving the chancellor's office, I'd felt like I was living in some kind of surreal counteruniverse. No fewer than a dozen people had come up and asked me about the video.

"*Attention.*" The voice came, fuzzy and too loud. I held my breath, not sure of what I wanted to hear. "The final votes for the Lambert student council elections have been tallied, and we have our winners. The results are as follows. For the position of president, the winner is . . . Jason Weatherby."

Pause. Nobody in class knew what to do. A few people clapped, but there was an air of tension in the room. The video had been powerful. Very powerful, and people were wondering more about that than the election.

170

"For the position of vice president, the winner is . . . Brooke Naples."

I took a deep breath.

"For the position of treasurer, the winner is . . . Talbott Presley . . . otherwise known as . . . Elvis."

The class cheered after this announcement, and I realized that besides *us*, the rich kids, the brainiacs supported their own, and Elvis was definitely one of them. They had their lines of loyalty just like the Chamber did.

"For the position of secretary, we have a forced withdrawal from the race. Thomas Singletary won with the most votes, but due to disregard for election protocol, he has been removed. Michael Woodside will be our new secretary."

Silence. They didn't know Woodsie was on our side, and the collective tension in the room turned to gloom. I heard a couple of *no ways* after that, but kept my silence. They'd find out soon enough, and besides that, I didn't know what the hell was going to happen. The only thing I knew was that I was more concerned about what Singletary was going to do than what would happen to me.

But we'd won, and if this all worked out, I'd keep my word. I'd take down the Chamber.

CHAPTER THIRTY-ONE

"HE'S NOT DONE, you know."

I looked at Brooke. We sat in my car after school. Elvis was in the backseat, staring at the roof. "I agree with Brooke. He's a nut. You could tell in the office he went over the edge."

I nodded. "Can't really blame him."

Brooke shook her head. "He scares me, Jason. Something isn't right with him."

"I know. I just don't know what. I can't figure it out."

Elvis snorted. "And it's not just the school. It's Carter. More like a personal thing."

"He faked his records to get into Lambert."

"Really?"

I nodded. "Yeah. Almost like he's stalking Carter."

"Told you he's a nut," Elvis said.

My phone rang, and I opened it. It was my dad. "Hello?"

"You know it's me, son. We need to speak. Now."

"I take it the school called?"

"Yes. It seems that after I left, a video was played."

"I didn't do it."

"It doesn't matter."

I sighed. "Dad, please. I got into this mess, and I'll get out of it."

"It's beyond that. The chancellor wants a meeting. You, your mother, and I. He's talking about possible expulsion if the investigation shows you knew about the video."

"I'm sure you'll make it all go away, right?" I mocked.

"No. Not this time."

"I can't come home. Not now."

His voice lowered. "Jason . . ."

"No, Dad, I have to fix this. Somebody is going to get hurt, and I can't let it happen."

"Then I'm calling the chancellor back and contacting the police. This is not your business."

"What isn't?"

"This Thomas Singletary character. The chancellor told me there is trouble between Carter and him."

"It is my business. I helped make it all happen."

"Come home. Your mother is here, too, and I've promised her nothing will happen. Just talk. We'll let the authorities do their job, and we'll do ours."

"Dad, will you please just trust me? For once?"

"Jason, Chancellor Patterson told me how Thomas was behaving in his office. He believes the boy to be . . . on the edge. He said he was threatening. Come home."

173

I paused. "Sorry, Dad, I can't." Then I closed the phone.

Brooke looked at me. "Wow. Did you really just do that?"

"I guess so."

"What are you going to do?"

"I don't know. I've got to think."

"You think Thomas will really hurt Carter?"

"He already broke his arm."

Elvis cut in. "Yeah, but just like he said, that was payback for ordering his arm busted. Not just out of nowhere."

I stared out the windshield. "Yeah. Payback." A moment passed. "Listen, I've got to go." I looked at Brooke. "Call me later?"

"Jason . . ."

I smiled. "I just blew my dad off, Brooke. You really think you're going to change my mind?"

Elvis guffawed. "I don't think so."

I nodded. "Don't worry. It'll work out. I just have to talk to Thomas."

"That's all?"

"Yes."

"Promise?"

"Yes."

She smiled. "You're a horrible liar."

I shrugged. "That's not fair. I have no idea if I'll even be able to find him, and if I do, how could I know what would happen?"

"Maybe your dad is right, then. Just call the police."

I fired the engine up. "Maybe he is right, but I'm a part of this. I brought Thomas into this deal."

She opened the door. "Call me later? Please?"

"Sure."

She leaned over and kissed me. I kissed her back. She smiled. "Does this mean, you know, that we're together?"

Elvis groaned. "Emotional exchanges make me claustrophobic. Let me out."

Brooke moved her seat forward. Elvis got out. She turned to me. "So?"

I smiled. "So I'd love that."

"Not just because you saw me half-naked?"

"No. I promise." Then I kissed her again.

She got out of the car. "I hope you know I'm calling the police about this, just like the school. And your dad. Everybody is right, Jason. He's dangerous."

"If I find him and things are bad, I'll call them myself."

CHAPTER THIRTY-TWO

As I DROVE, I thought about Thomas. Everything he'd done and said flashed through me, and there was something nagging at the edge of my mind. The poster. That was it. The poster of Carter's father. Then the vodka with the shot glass. There was a connection there, and it was more than just humiliating Carter because his dad was a drunk. There was something else, too. It was too coincidental that Carter had picked Thomas for me to get rid of. Whatever I didn't know, Carter did, and he'd known it all along.

I hung a right and gunned it, shifting through the gears to the sound of the engine screaming, and flew down Dudley Avenue, braking hard when I reached the public-library parking lot.

Inside, I found a free computer and sat down, glancing at my watch. Six-thirty. With a few clicks, I accessed the local newspaper archives and put a search in for Judge Logan. Years of stories showed up; page after page of news, judgments, verdicts, and rulings. I began as far back as the records went, scrolling, reading quickly, scanning for names. An hour passed and I'd only gotten through half of them.

My eyes burned from concentrating, and then I hit it. The headline read "Judge Carter Logan Charged with DUI." As I read the details of the arrest, I blinked, and my heart fluttered. The nightclub, the Blue Sapphire, was mentioned. Judge Logan had been driving home after a night of heavy drinking, and in the process had crashed his car, severely injuring a pedestrian. Reading further, I learned that the judge made a statement to police that the pedestrian had been crossing the street illegally and he'd not seen him. He refused to blow into a Breathalyzer, and was booked for driving under the influence. Blood tests conducted at the station were pending, and possible driving while intoxicated charges were awaiting complete analysis.

I clicked out and scrolled down, seeing another headline. It read "Local Judge Charged with DUI, Reckless Endangerment After Hitting Pedestrian." The person was listed in critical condition at Holy Family Hospital and was in a coma due to severe head trauma. He'd been walking to his car after a late night at work as an electrical engineer, drawing up plans for a new museum to be built honoring local war veterans.

The next article was "Man Dies, Judge Logan Charged with Involuntary Manslaughter." My stomach shriveled as I read: "The man, David Clinton Singletary, 42 and the father of two, succumbed to injuries suffered in the incident. His wife of thirteen years, Kimberly Singletary, said he was 'dedicated to his family, a good dad and a wonderful husband. He will be missed.'"

It went on to say that Judge Logan was freed on his own

recognizance, which was rare in such cases, but due to his standing in the community, he wasn't considered a flight risk. I sighed.

Judge Logan killed Thomas Singletary's father.

I scrolled down to the next article, and it hit me like a double-barreled shotgun blast to the chest. "District Attorney Drops All Charges but One in Logan Manslaughter Case." It stated that because the booking officer had not properly submitted the blood-alcohol report, there were no grounds to charge anything other than reckless endangerment. Manslaughter charges were dropped due to the pedestrian's jaywalking at night; the investigation claimed that Mr. Singletary had been crossing the street illegally, two feet outside the crosswalk lines. Judge Logan's attorneys had agreed to one year of rehabilitation and one year of community service. No trial had been held.

It all fit.

And now I knew why Thomas had traded out justice for payback, because there was no justice. Just a kid who'd lost a great dad and watched as the world ignored it. Watched as the powerful rolled a pair of loaded dice.

I knew then that Thomas Singletary was dangerous. *Very* dangerous. Not just on the edge, but over it. I reasoned that if he'd go to the extreme pains of hacking school records to get into Lambert, bugging the Chamber, breaking Carter's arm, and orchestrating that election video, the kid had *never* planned on Carter Logan's simply being humiliated, ruined, and run out of Lambert. I shuddered.

He wanted to kill him.

CHAPTER THIRTY-THREE

I KNOCKED THE CHAIR over as I bolted from the library, digging for my keys and hopping in the Mustang. I blistered the pavement on the way out, skinning tracks of rubber as I shifted, smoke pouring from the tires. I had to get to him. To stop him.

Thomas wasn't stupid. The endgame was here, and time was running out. The police had been contacted, and they'd be looking for him. And if they didn't get to him before he got to Carter, it would be over. Finished.

It would be tonight. Somehow, somewhere, it would be tonight.

I came to a stop in front of his apartment building and jumped out, running into the lobby and dashing down the hall. I knocked on the door. A moment later, it opened. A woman, slight, tired-looking, and with her hair braided, gazed at me.

"Mrs. Singletary?"

She was wary, uncertainty in her eyes. "Yes?"

"My name is Jason Weatherby. Is Thomas here?"

She paused, hesitant, then looked down the hall. "No. Why?"

"I need to see him. Do you know where he is?"

She stepped back, opening the door farther. "Are you one of his friends?"

"Yes. Sort of. We go to school together."

Nothing followed the question in her eyes. A moment passed. "Will you please come in?"

I took a breath. "I really need to talk to him, ma'am. If you could just tell me . . ."

"Come in."

I nodded.

As she led me in, I noticed the place was immaculate. Sparse, almost bare, and lit by a single lamp in the corner, it wasn't what I'd expected, and I felt like a judgmental fool. I heard the muffled sound of a television coming from a bedroom to the left. Mrs. Singletary took a seat on the couch. "Why do you need to see my son?"

"I go to school with him."

She nodded. "So you said. Please answer me."

"We're running for student council together, and I just . . ."

She shook her head. I stopped speaking. She frowned. "Three hours ago, the police knocked on my door asking the same as you. I'd appreciate your honesty, young man."

I grunted. There was nothing to lose but time, and I didn't have any. "Thomas faked his records to get into Lambert, and he's sort of got it in for another guy there. They don't like each other."

"I know."

I screwed my eyes at her. "You knew he faked his way into Lambert?"

"I didn't know that, but the police told me about this trouble." She paused. "Thomas always received high marks, and when he said he'd been accepted to Lambert, I didn't have reason to think it wasn't legitimate. I should have been more involved, but I have . . ." She looked away. "It's been difficult since his father passed."

"I'm sorry."

She cleared her throat. "Thomas has changed, and I work so much I'm simply not able to keep track of his life any longer. Will you please tell me what's going on? The police don't even know why."

"Didn't the chancellor call you?"

She shook her head. "I called the school after the police left in hopes that somebody would still be there. The chancellor was. Apparently, Thomas falsified our phone number in the school directory."

"What did the chancellor tell you?"

"He explained that the other boy's name was Carter." She looked away, and her words trailed off.

"Do you know who he is?"

She shook her head.

I took a breath. "His last name is Logan."

She stared at me for a moment, then tears formed in her eyes. "Oh God."

I realized then that this woman was owed much more than just the truth, but the truth was the only thing I could give. "I think Thomas is planning on killing Carter as payback. That's why I need to find him."

A moment passed. "He wouldn't do that." She looked at me. "He's a good boy. He's angry, yes, but . . ."

"He already broke Carter's arm. I've got to find him."

She swallowed, gaining her composure. "I don't know where he is."

I stood. "I'd better go."

"This is not your fault. It's mine. I didn't know how to deal with his hate, so I ignored it. I hoped he'd come out of it."

"I should go."

She sniffed, lowering her head. "This is my fault."

I had nothing to say to that, so I left.

CHAPTER THIRTY-FOUR

I SAT IN THE PARKING lot of Lambert, hidden in the darkest corner and away from the lamps casting circles of light on the pavement. I watched thousands of moths under those lights, drawn away from the darkness and toward the heat. Get too close and you die, I thought. Burnt alive. I'd driven by the Logan house and had seen nothing out of the ordinary as I studied the grounds in the darkness, even sneaking around back to peek in windows.

If it would happen, I thought, it would happen here at Lambert. In the Chamber.

I opened the car door and gently shut it, looking around the parking lot as I made my way toward the courtyard. The night was silent but for the fading buzz of the lights as I circled the main building, heading toward the spot where a little-known key to the gymnasium side door was hidden. It was gone, and my heart skipped a beat.

I stepped up to the door and turned the handle. Unlocked. I opened it, slipping in quietly and easing it closed.

"Quite a little display with the video today."

I spun, and Kennedy stood in the shadows of the hall, his bulk dark and menacing. I stepped back. "Yeah, it was."

He grinned. "I thought I looked pretty damn good on camera."

I ignored him. "I take it Carter is here."

He nodded.

"With Thomas?"

"You got it."

"And you?" I said.

He smiled again, menace in his eyes. "I'm here for you."

I squinted. "Did Carter set this meeting up, or Thomas?"

"Does it matter? Carter has a beef with the kid, and he's taking care of it. I, on the other hand, have a beef with you."

"Kennedy, this is serious. It's not a game anymore."

He grunted. "I don't really care, man. I'm just here to kick your ass."

"Why? Because Carter said so?" I smirked. "You know what he thinks of you, man. You're a tool. The guy laughs at you every time you turn your back."

He set his jaw. "Fuck off, Jason."

I shook my head. "Singletary isn't playing the game, Kennedy. He's over the edge, and you know Carter is, too." I pointed to the stairs. "One of them is going to end up dead."

Kennedy paused, and I could almost hear the wheels grinding in his thick skull.

I went on. "Judge Logan killed Singletary's father in a drunk-driving accident. He killed him and nothing happened. No jail,

184

no nothing." I stared at him. "Singletary wants payback." I sighed. "He broke Carter's arm, left the bottle, did the poster, made the video, did it all. And now he wants to kill him."

Kennedy's brutish face looked confused.

I stepped forward. "Think about it! It's like a fucked-up thing in his head. He wants Judge Logan to be hurt as much as he was hurt. Don't you get it?"

"That's twisted."

I shook my head. "Listen, I know you like doing shit like this, but do you really want to be a part of what's going to happen up there? Is it worth it?"

He stared.

"The guy even hacked his test scores to get into Lambert. He's off the charts."

"You're full of it."

"Dude, I know he hacked your psych records. That's why you stay away from him. You're even scared of the guy, so don't pretend anymore."

Silence.

"I haven't told anybody and don't plan on it, but I'm not lying here. His dad was a great guy, man, and Thomas is totally bent about it. He wants revenge. That's why he's done all of this."

He hesitated. "I don't have anything to do with who wants to kill who."

"You will if you don't get out of my way." I looked at him. "You going to let me pass?"

He stood his ground.

"You're not his slave, Kennedy. Jesus, use your head."

Silence.

Every nerve ending in my body was itching. Time was running out. "I'm walking past you, Kennedy. Don't stop me."

He stepped aside. "I wasn't here, Weatherby. You hear me? I let you pass, I was never here. In fact, I don't know a thing about what's going on. Deal?"

"Deal," I said as I rushed up the steps.

CHAPTER THIRTY-FIVE

I CREPT UP THE STAIRS, walked down the hall, and entered the main building. The doors to the Chamber were closed, and as I neared them, I stopped, taking my phone out. I texted Brooke and my dad: Call the police. They're in the Chamber.

I put my phone on vibrate and slipped it into my pocket. The carpeted hall was dark, the only light coming from a sconce next to the Chamber doors as I reached them. I swallowed, putting my ear to the wood and listening for a moment. Nothing. Then I pushed one door.

As the heavy oak swung open silently, I stepped back.

The first thing I saw was blood on the floor. Then I saw Singletary. He held the lead pipe. At his feet lay Carter Logan. Eyes closed, sprawled on his side. I could have thought he was sleeping but for the blood leaking from his ear.

Thomas raised his head, looking at me. His eyes were vacant.

As dead as his father. He furrowed his brow, then faced me. "You really shouldn't have come here, Jason."

I held up my hand. "Whoa. Slow down, Thomas. This can work out. It can."

"It is working out."

My mind raced. I glanced at Carter. His chest moved. "That's enough, Thomas. You proved your point. You got payback. It's done. And we won the election. We can change things."

He shook his head. "It's not done."

"I know about your father. I know why you're doing this."

He stared.

I nodded. "I know, and I understand. I do. And I know you want to kill him, but you can't."

"You don't understand anything." He shifted, standing over Carter again.

"I called the police. They're on the way. Don't do it."

He laughed, his words just above a whisper. "I'm not fucking stupid, Jason. I know where I'm going."

"Put the pipe down. Please," I said. He raised the pipe, leaning over Carter and getting ready to swing. My heart leaped, and the words came out in a gush. "What if your dad was here? Would he do it, Thomas? Would he? Would he wreck his own life because of scum like that?" I jabbed a finger at Thomas. "You were right. Sometimes there is no justice, but why ruin yourself because of it? Why let them ruin you? Why prove them right?"

He stopped moving, the pipe still raised as he stared at Carter. I almost dove for him, but I knew that if he nailed me, Carter would be done. We'd both be done. And in a strange way, it pissed me off. Really pissed me off. My dad made people

188

like Thomas, but Thomas made people like my dad. It was like a snake eating its own tail, and it made me sick with rage. "You know what, Thomas? You *are* fucking stupid. A stupid scumbag with nothing better to do than be pissed off at the world. You sit there and tell me that I can't change anything, and you walk around with all this shit in you, but you just make it worse! You kill him and everybody will think the same thing. Just another unhinged kid. Some loser with loser parents. Probably addicts. Well, screw you. You don't give a shit about your father or your mother or your sister or how they'll be seen if you do this. You only care about you, and you're too chicken to do anything else but keep on hurting the people you should be taking care of."

He clenched his teeth. "Shut your mouth."

"OR WHAT?" The words echoed I yelled them so loudly. I went on. "Or what, Thomas? You'll kill me, too? You think I'm here because I give a crap what happens to Carter? For some stupid reason, I like you." I paused, then went on. "I talked to your mom. Your dad was a good man. He loved his family. He loved you. He was killed by a drunk judge and it was wrong and everything else was wrong, and you're right. The world sucks. But that's what happens sometimes, and that's why you need to put that pipe down, because you're not changing anything. You're making yourself the same as them, and if your dad was alive . . ." I trailed off, the words disappearing. "You're hurting him as much as you're hurting yourself, Thomas, and you know it."

His face broke, just for a moment. "They don't care, man. None of them."

"I know. But I do. And your mom and sister do."

He set his chin, gripping the pipe harder. "He was a nothing to them."

"Put the pipe down."

He stared at me. "Tell me I'm wrong and I'll put the pipe down. Tell me I haven't been right all along."

I swallowed. I knew he was right, but there had to be a way. "I don't know, but . . ."

His faced twisted, and he brought the pipe down, smashing Carter on the shoulder. I sprang forward as he swung again, grabbing his arm, but he slithered away, jumping back and threatening me with the pipe. His face was a knot of pent-up rage and pain and horror, and tears streamed down his face. "WHY, JASON?" he screamed. "WHY? Why is it this way? Why did he die? How can there be people like this?"

I swallowed. "I don't know. But you're not this way. You're not like them. And I'm here as your friend. Nothing else."

He shook his head. "It's too late. Too late."

"No it's not."

He grunted, staring at Carter. "I'm done, man. Look at him."

"No you're not. Just pay the consequences and move on, Thomas. That's all. Please, I'm begging you. Stop."

He kept his eyes on Carter, who moaned.

I pointed. "He's the nothing, Thomas. And they'll all win if you do this. All of them."

His face was pained and tense, full of anger and indecision. For a moment, I could almost see the boy that lost his father, but then he blinked, his eyes turning cold.

"I won't let you, Thomas. You can kill me, but I won't let you."

He looked up at me. "Why?"

"Because you're a good person. Messed up, but good. Your mom showed me that, and now you need to show your dad you are."

Moments passed, and Thomas wiped his face with his sleeve. His eyes met mine. "I hate this world." Then he dropped the pipe.

EPILOGUE

CARTER LOGAN SUFFERED a cracked skull, two broken ribs, and multiple bruises. He spent a week in the hospital, then a month at home recuperating. No charges were filed concerning what had been shown on the video. He was expelled from Lambert, though.

Thomas was charged with aggravated assault with a deadly weapon, and was sentenced to seven months in juvenile detention, then probation until he turned eighteen.

I visit him every week. He's in counseling and anger-management classes, but he's still pissed. I think he'll always be.

My father is living with us again. My mom demanded counseling for all of us, as a family. He agreed, but he didn't like it. You should see him sitting in the shrink's office. He looks like a toy poodle shivering and shaking he's so uncomfortable, but it proved one thing to me. He loves my mom. Maybe even me.

And he's getting better. He took me aside the other day and told me he was proud. I believed it. He also told me that the speech I gave in the auditorium that day reminded him of why he'd gotten into politics. Wow. I never thought I'd hear anything like that from him.

Oh yeah, the election. We kept our promises. Lambert is the way it should be, or most of the way, anyhow, and Chancellor Patterson actually shook my hand three days ago in the hall. We're in the process of reorganizing the Youth Leadership Group, and we'll hold votes in the next week. Parents are screaming about it, but there's nothing they can do about this little thing we call democracy. The only one I feel sorry for is the chancellor, because he's the one taking the heat.

I'll be leaving Lambert at the end of the year. I don't belong there, and my mom agreed to let me transfer to another school. A public school. I plan on studying construction management in college. My dad disagrees, but he's learning that I'm not him.

Thomas Singletary taught me a big lesson in life, and I'm grateful for it. But he still scares the hell out of me. His father's death damaged him, but I'm hoping the counseling will help. His justice isn't the kind I believe in, but it's hard to dispute his rage, because the system I want so much to believe in is messed up. Those lines of power need to be there, but he helped me see that sometimes they get directed in a way that does more damage than good. My dad is a perfect example of that.

More than anything, I wish life could be simple. I wish Thomas and I could be closer friends. I wish Carter wasn't insane. I wish guys like Michael Woodside who know what's right and want to do right didn't have to play the game to survive. I wish Kennedy would voluntarily staple his mouth shut.

I guess I wish the world could be the way it is when I'm with Brooke. Sweet. I'm taking her out for burgers later, and the most popular kid at Lambert is joining us. Yeah. Elvis. You rock.

ACKNOWLEDGMENTS

I'd like to thank Kimberly Harmon. The strongest woman I know. George Nicholson, my agent. No words from a high school dropout can describe my respect for you. Thanks, George. Joan Slattery, senior executive editor, Alfred A. Knopf Books for Young Readers, my fantastic and so cool editor, thank you. My thanks also go to Erin Clarke, executive editor, Alfred A. Knopf Books for Young Readers. I'd also like to thank every person out there who has done what they know is right. Even if it hurts to do it.

ABOUT THE AUTHOR

Michael Harmon was born in Los Angeles and now lives in the Pacific Northwest. He dropped out of high school as a senior and draws on many of his experiences in his award-winning fiction for young adults.

To learn more about Michael Harmon and his books, please visit booksbyharmon.com.